Tangled Spells

Witches of Willow Creek
Tangled Magic Series: Book 4
Denise D. Young

eISBN: 978-1-956327-02-1

print ISBN: 978-1-956327-03-8

Cover Design by Victoria Cooper Art.

Part One: Prophecies

"For words, like Nature, half reveal
And half conceal the Soul within."
— Alfred Lord Tennyson

Chapter One

Siobhan

Willow Creek, Virginia

The summer day had broken golden and mauve, a bit of peacefulness in the midst of trouble. Morning sunlight sparkled over the dewy fields below, but even a gorgeous morning full of wildflowers and birdsong couldn't hide the troubles in store for me.

Magic.

That was the trouble.

That was *always* the trouble.

Yet another battle that pitted human against fae, witch against immortal.

I flew over the farmhouses, following the meandering path of Willow Creek far below, where its clear waters babbled across rocks. In my raven form, the mystical energies of the land felt even more askew.

Yeah, the witches of Willow Creek were in way too deep, way over their precious mortal heads.

You have to come to Willow Creek. Those had been my great-uncle's words four months ago. *It's time.*

The magic here is sick. The elementals have vanished. The signs... His voice had broken.

Uncle Mick had been scarcely more than a boy when he'd moved to America with nothing more than a rucksack and a guitar case. Willow Creek was his home, the family cottage in Ireland now a distant memory for him. He'd built his house

2

here with the help of friends while tending bar and saving every penny he could. He'd taught folk songs and talked about his motherland to anyone who was willing to lend an ear.

Yeah, he loved Willow Creek as much as he'd loved Ireland. Voice cracking, he'd finished, *The signs are clear. It's happening. Ask the Rose. Go to the well and seek the Rose.*

And dammit, to hear his voice like that...I'd asked. I'd sat at the edge of the well and made my offering. The Rose was the eldest of the earthbound fae, those who'd stayed behind in the human realm after the divide. The Rose was the sort of creature who my family revered but always made my stomach roil, my voice squeak, and my palms sweaty.

But I'd gone to her, sat on the edge of her well and asked. With grim honesty, her green gaze had fixed me, and she'd answered.

I'd even gone to Dublin, where I asked a witch's tarot pack.

And every time the question left my lips, the answer was the same.

I had to go to Willow Creek.

So, I came. I came, I waited tables at Uncle Mick's pub, the local live-music go-to joint called The Thirsty Fiddler...and I waited for an opening.

And the whole time, I lied. About who I was. About my allegiances. About my agenda. And whose side I was *really* on.

Today the sky was clear, dew sparkling on the mountains below. From my vantage point, cool air beneath my inky wings, I could see far into the distance, where bluish mountains seemed to stretch on forever.

But beneath the beauty, a sickness waited. Every day since I'd set foot in Willow Creek, I felt it. It seeped into me, set my teeth on edge.

If I were a witch, my human side would be enough to block it out—most of the time, at least.

But I wasn't a witch, just a fae-woman passing for one.

So, yeah, you bet your sweet ass I couldn't forget.

The air tingled across my feathers, a memory of a thousand spells. The Willow Creek Coven had been influencing the magic of this place longer than even they knew. Two-hundred years, easy.

The fae magic of the place was older. It always was. Ancient, beyond time. A set of legends, of songs and stories repeating throughout time.

Long before the Willow Creek Coven cast its first spell, the fae had been here. Protecting the land and its powerful nexus of magic. There were many such places, scattered across the world. Each sacred, each unique. Each carefully guarded by the fae.

But in Willow Creek, the fae had let down their guard, abandoned their post.

And the cost would be high.

A gust of wind battered me, and with a caw of irritation, I made my way back to Uncle Mick's place, landing on the railing of his cedar deck, clutching the reddish wood with my talons.

Mick, leaned over the railing, staring at the mountain view he swore never got old, and chuckled. "You need to stop flying around like that. You're going to scare the pants off some superstitious old lady."

In a swirl of lights, I transformed back into my regular self—right down to the jeans and bell-sleeve peasant top I'd donned that morning. Being a fae shifter had added benefits human shifters didn't have. Like keeping my clothes and jewelry through a shift.

I readjusted my labradorite pendant and frowned at him. "As usual, Uncle Mick, I feel like you're referencing something, but I don't know what."

He chuckled again and took a swig from his mug. "There's an old rhyme about crows. *One for sorrow*, it goes..."

I dropped my pendant and crossed my arms over my chest, shooting him a glare. "I am not a crow. I am a raven."

He jutted his chin toward the sky. "From that height, most folks can't tell. They just see an unfortunate omen."

I sighed. "I didn't bring this down on Willow Creek. I'm just here to stop it."

Uncle Mick crossed the porch and dropped a paternal kiss on my cheek. "And so you shall, dear Siobhan. And so you must." He stepped back. "How did it go last night? Did their spell work?"

Ah. The real reason he was waiting for me out here. A status report. I turned to stare at an aged oak tree in the otherwise open yard. In its shade, two blue jays bickered over the contents of a birdfeeder while a squirrel watched from the branches, no doubt waiting for his chance at the contents of the feeder my uncle filled nightly.

"They solved the riddlebound. I did as I was instructed. I acted as a guide. I earned the trust of some of the coven members."

"Some?" Mick loaded the single word with an edge of disappointment. "Let me guess. Nicholas doesn't trust you."

I tucked my short blond hair behind my ear and leaned my back against the porch railing. "It's not my fault. I'm not, what you would call, Miss Congeniality. I wasn't raised to be some sort of faerie ambassador. You can't expect me to magically become one. That isn't how magic works."

Sweet Goddess Anu. I was a grown woman—twenty-two years old. And yet this mission—and the entire family's meddling in my role in it—made me feel like a petulant child.

"No one expects you to be that, Siobhan. I know how your training works. I know what you were raised for—exactly as the Rose prophesized."

"Yeah," I muttered. No one ever deviated. My whole life, mapped out in the stars before I was even born. "Exactly as she planned."

Mick squeezed my shoulder. He was a burly sort of man—not tall, but strong, a man who'd spent his entire life playing music, writing songs, and tending bar. Even in his seventies, he could pick up a bin full of dirty dishes as effortlessly as a younger man could wield an empty tray.

He'd been given a choice at a young age: music or immortality. He'd chosen music.

At least you had a choice, I wanted to snap.

The family barked orders.

I followed.

And then they wondered why I was less than diplomatic. The family curmudgeon, from the time I was a child.

"I'll tell you what," Mick said, stroking his chin. "I think you and Nick Felson could relate to one another. He never took to magic the way his brother did. Maybe resented it a little. You might find you have something in common with the coven's new high priest."

"And his girlfriend?" I reminded my uncle. "She has the Kenning. She knows I'm not who I say I am. I see it in her eyes when she looks at me. If the high priest and priestess of the coven don't trust me, they're not going to let me in. Period."

At that moment, I wished that I could assume my raven form and fly across the Virginia, soar over the churning waters of the Atlantic, land amid the craggy rocks and ancient trees of home, and go strolling back in the door of the family cottage.

But even my magic had its limits.

"Siobhan, you have a genuineness about you people like. And you are a gifted storyteller. Tell a story. Let it come from your heart. Not everything about you has to be hidden here. Not everything you say must be a lie."

A gust of wind blew my short, chunky bob-cut hair across my face. With a huff I pushed it away.

"Fine. I'll make some of Aunt Fiona's scones to take over to the farm." Best get this over with, right?

Mick chuckled. "Already done, along with some raspberry preserves."

"Stop chuckling," I said, irritated. "I'm not that bad of a cook."

His chuckle became a full-out belly laugh.

"Oh, for Anu's sake," I griped, but I couldn't help the smile that crept onto my face. I tossed up my hands. "I'm going, okay. I'm going."

I stepped into the kitchen of my uncle's mountaintop cabin and grabbed the basket from the counter.

That was the thing about Mick O'Shea.

The man had a joy that was bloody freaking contagious.

With my head held high, I grabbed the keys to the pickup truck and headed out the door.

To pretend I was a witch in the worst place to play pretend: a coven whose members were fighting for their very existence.

Oh, yeah. May the goddess Anu, mother of the fae, bless my soul.

***

Weir

Mountain Pass, Winter Realm of the Fae

I ducked behind a pale gray stone, heart hammering, scarcely daring to breath in case I was heard.

On the other side, a trio of fae strode past, daggers of obsidian belted at their waists, their deep blue cloaks pulled up over their faces.

I waited, still as the boulder that hid my shivering form, until they passed. If they stopped, they'd only see a hunched figure, clad in the same gear they wore, but if they came close enough, they'd sense I wasn't one of their own.

Not a fae man, but a witch—a human man with a bit of magic, a trespasser in the Winter Realm of the fae.

I waited behind the stone until they passed. I'd been lucky once, early in my journey through the pass, to acquire the few meager items I had with me: the cloak, which seemed to be woven with an enchantment that kept out the worst of the wintry chill, and a cauldron that could produce a meager but sustaining meal several times a day.

If I never ate potato soup or rye bread for the next thousand years, it would still be too soon.

The trio passed, and after giving them a few minutes, I continued on my way, thankful that they'd been heading in the opposite direction.

To say the Mountain Pass of the Winter Realm was an unforgiving place would be the understatement of the century. I'd been wandering the pass for weeks now, since I'd managed to escape my imprisonment. I didn't know if the six other coven members who Weylin had taken hostage—including my younger sister and my mother—were still imprisoned in the enchanted tree where Weylin held them captive.

Only the unwavering belief that I'd somehow know if they were gone kept me certain they were alive.

Witch's intuition, my mom called it.

Three months ago, the trapped coven had managed to cast a spell that brought the mystical walls of our prison down for a split second. I made it through. The others did not.

The plan was to escape the Winter Realm and get help somewhere. We didn't know if other fae were in league with Weylin, our captor. We didn't know if he'd gone rogue or if he had taken our coven with the approval—or at the behest—of the Winter Queen herself.

Our high priestess, Ginny's, words came thundering back to me. "Whoever gets out that door, trust no one. We know there are doors in this realm. We know that in this realm, those doors are rarely visible. Be strong, and find a doorway back to Willow Creek."

That night we'd cast the spell, from within in a stone tower where winds wailed and winter wolves howled, a full moon had cast silvery light on the snow and the yew trees around us.

We'd given every ounce of our magic.

It had worked. For a brief, flickering second, the doors had been flung open. I'd tried to grab my sister's hand, to pull her out with me.

But the door shut before I could pull her through, magic sealing it closed.

"Run! Weir, go, before he comes back!" My sister, Winnie, had screamed at me, giving me a shove.

She'd been right.

I'd made a choice. If Weylin had returned and found me outside, he would've killed me, if only to serve as an example to the others.

Fortunately, I'd been a cross-country runner in high school and then in college. I could've run faster and farther in my puma shifter form, but I hadn't dared to shift—our high priestess, Ginny, had warned me that my shifter magic might not be reliable or safe in the Faerie Realms.

But even in my human form, I was good at running. And so, I ran.

I'd been on the run ever since that night, in a place where the seasons never changed, where winter's bite never gave way to the promise of spring.

It was just this. Ice and sleet, snow and wind, and the high gray mountains of jagged rock that never seemed to lead anywhere but deeper into the pass.

Truth was, I was lost. If there was a door, I was starting to doubt I'd ever find it. I needed a miracle, and even in this realm of pure magic, my chances of finding one looked grim.

A gust of wind sent my hood tumbling backward. I tugged it back over my face and pushed forward, looking for a hidden nook to stop and rest for the night.

I wanted to believe that somehow I would find a way out of the Mountain Pass: a doorway, a spell, a sigil, a border with another realm. I clung to hope I would find something, a glimpse of sunshine or scent of wildflowers in this cold, barren place.

But that wasn't happening tonight, so it was time to look for a place to rest, eat a bit, sleep a bit, before I kept trudging on.

And honestly, unless something changed, I was starting to think I would be wandering this icy pass forever.

Chapter Two

Siobhan

The gravel driveway and surrounding grass were full of parked cars as I pulled up to the Felson family farm. My stomach fluttered. I gritted my teeth against the sensation and snatched up the basket.

All of those cars? They meant the *entire* Willow Creek Coven was here—or at least, those members who weren't trapped in some fae-magicked prison in the Winter Realm of the fae folk.

I wasn't much for purses, but I'd started carrying a charcoal gray mini-backpack that I kept a few provisions in. Almost everything inside was magical in nature, aside from my passport, debit card, and a tube of rosy red lip gloss. But there was something else I hoped to add to the bag today.

Something currently in Evan Felson's possession. Something I needed to make the next step of the Rose's plan happen.

My stomach twisted further as I remembered the sight of Evan's hand retreating from that glimmering pool of magic, clutching that velvet pouch, removing the golden key from within.

A riddlebound. Powerful fae magic, but something that even I, a faerie myself, had only heard of in lore and never seen. A tiny pocket in the astral realm where a hidden object was kept concealed. In this case, that object was a key—a key to an enchanted doorway behind which the missing coven members were imprisoned.

Today's meeting of the magical minds was about how to proceed.

We'd solved the riddlebound and found the key. Now, we had to figure out how to use the damn thing.

And all of that before the black moon—tomorrow night, at midnight. The Rose had told me as much, and the coven had procured the same information from various sources.

I steeled myself and walked in, trying to seem casual. My cousins often informed me that my attempts at seeming casual, calm, and collected instead came off rather distant and snooty, but it was the best I could manage. You know, trying to project a this-is-me-deal-with-it air while my insides felt like gelatin.

"Standard Siobhan," my cousin Deirdre called it playfully.

Home. I missed my cousins and their playful banter, a place where a girl could drop her guard and simply be. I missed the way the trees whispered their secrets while I perched in their branches in my raven form, and my auntie's cottage across the way where a damned good cup of tea could always be found.

But I was far from home, so I tucked my hair behind my ear and raised my hand to knock.

The back door of the yellow farmhouse creaked open before I could rap my knuckles against it.

Cassie stood there, short and willowy, her blond hair flowing down to her waist, two small sections clipped back with a wooden butterfly clip, looking every bit the 1970s waif she was.

A chorus of "morning's" and "hey's" greeted me as Cassie ushered me inside. Only Nick Felson, Cassie's boyfriend and Evan's twin brother, looked suspicious of my presence.

When I'd arrived earlier in the summer, the only remaining coven member had been Nick. I'd tried to make friends with him on the rare occasion he'd come into the Thirsty Fiddler, Uncle Mick's pub slash music venue, but he wasn't interested.

Then a spell awoke Cassie from a forty-five year slumber, and the magical energy shifted. Her awakening in the twenty-first century would be the catalyst, the Rose had told me.

I forced a smile. "I brought scones!" I said, holding the basket up and dangling it promisingly from my fingers.

Bailee, a bubbly bookworm and the local librarian, enwrapped me in a hug and grabbed the basket. "Need!" she cried, peeling back the cheesecloth to reveal the goodies Mick had tucked inside. Clad in a magenta dress bedecked with pentacles, Bailee definitely wore her witchy status with beaming pride.

Evan gave me a friendly smile as he claimed a scone from the basket and passed it to the next person. With long hair and a definite indie-folk musician vibe, he was a contrast to his rather stoic twin.

Vi, a fire witch with faerie magic, was tall, with red hair and a smattering of freckles. Quiet with a hidden wisdom, today she wore a pair of teal leggings and a long black tank top, a blue lapis-lazuli crystal point dangling from a silver chain around her neck. Her fox-shifter boyfriend, Aiden, with his raven black hair and casual attire, completed the group.

Most covens consisted entirely of witches, but necessity was the mother of invention—wasn't that the saying? In order to save the Crossroads of Magic from some seriously deadly dark faerie magic, the Willow Creek Coven was rapidly adapting, opening their ranks to shifters and learning how to use the newfound faerie magic of some of their members.

They thought I was half-fae—like some of the members themselves. If they found out I was full-blooded fae? Well, even the most open-minded of covens wouldn't admit me into their ranks. Witches tended to use a proceed-with-caution approach with the fae. And with good reason.

Tricksters, they called us.

They weren't wrong.

Cassie slid a cup of tea into my hands. Somehow, she'd already added just the right amount of cream and sugar, and I took a sip, trying to ground myself the way Aunt Fiona had taught me.

Nick moved to the center of the crowded kitchen, clearing his throat. "Cassie and I have been talking about it. We don't think we can afford to wait until tonight to do the ritual."

Around the room, heads bobbed in agreement.

"Do we have a ritual written?" Bailee asked. "Because I found a book in Grams's library that might be useful." She grabbed an oversized tote bag and rummaged through, before pulling out a book with a deep purple cover emblazoned with a pattern of gold vines. It looked mass-produced here in the human realm, and while part of me doubted that it held anything useful, I knew that witches had managed to acquire quite a bit of knowledge on fae lore over the years.

Never underestimate a human, Mick had told me upon my arrival. *Especially not a witch.*

"Well, don't keep us in suspense," Aiden, the fox shifter, said. "What does it say?"

Bailee flipped through the book and read, "The fae are notorious for collecting treasures from the human realm. Keys, jewels, books, slippers, and all manner of items have gone missing for years, only to be returned when the human owner of the item made a series of offerings to the fae to return the item. But sometimes, a more direct approach must be taken, particularly when what goes missing isn't an object at all.

"The most famous case in modern memory is that of Biddy Marlowe, of Cornwall, in 1901. Rumored to be a witch blessed with faerie sight, Biddy witnessed the wee ones stealing her beloved familiar, a cat named Hermes, one October evening. After leaving the customary offerings of berries and cream—and even a beloved brooch—to appease the fae and solicit her familiar's return, Biddy took more drastic measures—"

"Wait." Nick held up a hand. "B, we're not talking about a missing cat. And Weylin didn't steal our slippers."

"Yeah," Cassie said, her tone more gentle. "I think the motivation of those fae was probably different. Are you sure this is going somewhere helpful?"

"I think it is." The words were soft, a few steps above a whisper, but all heads turned toward Vi. Her red hair fell over her shoulder. "The circumstances might be different, but the magic could easily be reworked to our situation."

"I just don't want to waste time—" Nick countered, crossing his arms over his chest.

"I don't either, Saint Nick," Bailee said. "My Grams is missing too. I'm trying to be *helpful*."

"Can you give us the abridged version, then?" Nick grumbled.

"Nick," Cassie said, her tone a soft warning.

"I think it's better if you know the full story..." Bailee countered. "I don't want to skip something that might be important."

The tension in the room was rising. I set my mug down, rubbing my temples. This was one of the many reasons I spent so little time among humans. I could feel everything. I ended up walking around like my nerve endings were raw and ragged.

"We can always—" Aiden said.

Just as Evan said, "I think she's on to—"

And Nick countered with, "We need to be getting the ritual—"

"Stop!" The word flew out of my mouth before I could stop it.

Everyone stopped talking. All eyes were on me in an instant. My face grew hotter than a Yule log on the winter solstice.

Nick locked eyes with me. "What do you think we should do, Siobhan?" His tone was calm, but I couldn't mistake the look in his eyes. Suspicion. He was testing me.

I stepped forward. Nick was far taller than I was, but with my fae magic, I could intimidate even the strongest of humans.

I tamped my magic back down. No. I was here to work with the coven, gain their trust. Not to scare them into submission.

"I'm familiar with the story of Biddy Marlowe. She used a form of magic mostly forgotten. Not even most human accounts fully capture the power of the ancient magic she used that night. Biddy was a widow. She'd lost her two sons to fever. She was shunned by her village. That cat was her only friend in the world—her only family. She would've moved heaven and earth to bring him back."

An expectant stillness filled the room.

Good. I had their attention.

I tilted my chin up, meeting Nick's steely gaze. "Like I said, she would've moved heaven and earth to bring her familiar—her only family—back. And, as story goes, she did. It started with a trip to a tea shop on the Cornish coast, where fae and witch frequently crossed paths..."

And I told them exactly how Biddy had brought Hermes back—with a bit of magical lore gifted to her by a faerie. Leaving out, of course, that the faerie woman who'd gifted Biddy the spell had been my aunt.

***

Weir

I blinked, my eyelids heavy, mind foggy with sleep. The air against my skin was surprisingly warm.

Too warm.

I scanned my surroundings. I was in a cavern, but it wasn't like the cold, barren ones that dotted the Mountain Pass. Last I remembered, I'd found one of those caves and settled in for the night.

This one, however, was cool but not cold, and teeming with life, despite an obvious lack of sunshine. Vines of deep green dotted with large crimson blooms climbed up the dark rock. Moss spotted a few of the rocks surrounding me, and a pool of crystalline water took up most of the space. Water dripped from stalactites above, the sound amplified in the cavern.

Wherever this was, it wasn't the Winter Realm of the fae. But both the witch and the shifter in me sensed deep magic stirring in every inch of the place, magic that was unlike the icy magic of winter. It felt...almost like home.

"Weir."

I turned as a figure appeared from one of the tunnels.

"Mom?"

My heart thudded. It felt like a lifetime ago since I'd left my mother and sister and the rest of the coven in that forsaken prison. I ran to her and wrapped her in an embrace, one powerful enough that I lifted her off her feet.

She chuckled. "I'm glad to see you too."

"I swear, I haven't given up. I'm trying so hard to get back to you, to save you."

"I know. Could you, uh, put me down?"

"Right. Sorry."

I set her down, taking a moment to look at her. I'd inherited her dark hair, as had my sister, and her lean, athletic build. My mom had been a marathon runner in her twenties and thirties, and I'd inherited her talents as a long-distance runner.

"What are you wearing?" I asked. Mom was nothing if not practical, favoring flannel shirts, t-shirts, and jeans. Instead, she wore a floor-length dress of pale blue, a wide ruffle at the top of the sleeveless gown.

She chuckled again. "I don't know. I didn't pick it. This place, the magic here, did. I guess it thought I needed to look the part."

I frowned, feeling my brow furrow.

She reached out, her calloused thumb smoothing my forehead. "You're going to get premature wrinkles if you keep scowling like that, you know." Her tone was kind, teasing.

"Well, what if you told me why we're here? And what this place is?"

"This place is the Crossroads of Magic—the nexus of magic that lies underneath Willow Creek. And the coven managed one more burst of magic to bring us together here."

"So, you're okay? You? And Winnie?" I never stopped thinking about my sister. Winnie's magic was powerful, but more curse than blessing. A gifted empath, being imprisoned so close to others had to be taking its toll.

Mom took my hand and gave it a squeeze. "We're both fine. Maeve and Ginny have experience working with empaths, and they're teaching her to control her abilities. In a way, she's stronger than ever. But you'll see soon enough. All we know, Weir, is that the next stage of our journey is in your hands. I could sense you were lost, needing guidance. That's why I'm here."

I did my best to unfurrow my stubborn brow. My mother might have been the most practical, down-to-earth person I knew—but she was also as gifted a seer as my sister was an empath.

"Is that your way of saying shut up and listen?"

Mom quirked an eyebrow, hand sweeping up to rest on her hip. "Maybe." She gestured toward the pool of glistening water.

"I'm told some scrying pools have moods, and that the colors of the waters change. From light to dark, from clear to cloudy, depending on their mood. The waters are clear and shining today." She nodded, the look on her face telling me she had made some sort of determination. "That's a good sign."

"Do I need to remind you that I'm no seer?" I prodded. When she shot me a sharp glance, I quickly added, "So maybe you could clue me in as to what we're doing here?"

Mom seized my hand and guided me toward the water. "Today, you are. You come from a family of seers, you know. I can see the future. Your grandmother could see it too. Winnie sees others' emotions—sometimes more clearly than they see them themselves."

"And I'm a shifter with a bit of witchcraft in my veins," I countered. "I can weave a little spell here or there, sure. But seeing?"

"Ginny and I have been talking. She thinks you have an untapped gift, that somehow your witchcraft and your shifter magic are entangled. You might have powers stronger than I do, you know. We just haven't figured out how to unlock them. This is just a glimpse, a shared vision to help you understand what's to come, to help you unlock that gift. I'll peer into the pool, which will allow you to see what I see. You'll witness my vision. With any luck, that will allow you to understand your magic better. And if you understand the true nature of your dual magicks..."

She smiled, that annoyingly knowing smile, and I knew it was my turn to speak.

"Then I can find a doorway out of the winter wonderland I've been trapped in?"

Her smile became a full-fledged grin, and she patted my hand. "Precisely."

It was a crazy plan. But I didn't need to tell Mom that. Mom didn't deal in crazy plans. Despite her magical gifts, Mom didn't do impractical. My dad was the inventor, the family creative. Mom was the pragmatic one, her farrier business carrying us through the rough times when Dad, ever-loving but head-in-the-clouds, was "between ideas."

"Mom? Is everything really okay? Is Winnie..."

Her hand came to rest on her hip again, and she cocked her head. "I wouldn't lie. Winnie is fine. She's learning to control her powers, finding strength within the coven. It's just...we're running out of time. I had a vision. It's bad. If the coven isn't re-united...we have hours. A day at most."

"Tell me." My voice was low, a deep rumble despite the lump forming in my throat. "Tell me what you saw."

Maybe she could show me. Here, in this place, that might be possible. But I wasn't so sure I wanted to see.

She didn't meet my gaze this time—never a good sign. "Ruin, my cub. Willow Creek, gone. The coven—all of us, both here and back home. Gone."

I nearly stumbled back, as if struck. We hadn't lived in Willow Creek long—a few years. But it was home. More importantly, it was full of innocent people, going about their lives. They didn't deserve any of this.

"Tell me, Mom," I whispered. "Am I the only one? Am I the only one who can save you?"

She squeezed my hand again. "That's what we're here to find out."

"I guess it's good then. That the waters are clear, I mean." I swallowed hard, fighting back that lump in my throat that was rapidly growing into a gnawing ache.

Mom's hair—predominantly gray with a few stubborn remnants of chestnut—flowed down her back, unrestrained. I stepped forward, stomach churning.

I'd meant what I said—I was no seer.

"Root deep into the earth, Weir," she whispered, her voice taking on that deep tone it did whenever she prepared to work magic. "Imagine tree roots, connecting you to the earth."

I squirmed. As many times as that phrase had been uttered in rituals and at magical gatherings, I'd never connected to it. Sure, my magic was of the earth, but the puma in me couldn't imagine the sense of stillness she described.

"Focus," Mom said, in that voice that made me feel like a six-year-old who wouldn't sit still for my cousin's dance recital.

I sighed. The weight of everything threatened to crash down on me. Not just the fate of my family hung in the balance. Not just the fate of my coven. But of Willow Creek. Its magic. And possibly its inhabitants.

I itched to run, to shift and keep running, to run so hard the Winter Realm disappeared into a gray blur.

That wasn't an option.

I pressed my eyelids tighter together.

Goddess of Wild Things, let me see.

Reluctantly, I let them flutter open.

Mom smiled at me again. She released my hand.

"Goddess of Wild Things," she cried, raising her hands toward the sky. "Let him see. Lend my power to him, in this space between the worlds. Let him see."

Energy crackled in the air. The hairs on my arms and the back of my neck stood on end.

I gazed into the pool, its waters sparkling, shimmering, silvery-blue now.

A door. Vibrant blue, like the sapphire in Mom's anniversary band Dad gave her for their twenty-fifth.

Like watching a movie that was slightly out of focus, I peered into the waters.

The door vanished. In its place, a flurry of black feathers. A raven, perching on a branch covered in deep-green leaves, its amber eyes locking with mine.

A shiver went down my spine. A sense of familiarity and...how could I describe it?

Fated rightness, my animal instincts declared—not in a mere whisper, but a full guttural cry.

The raven disappeared. In its place, a temple built of glistening golden stone, surrounded by a sea of red lilies. A woman stepped forward. Her hair was blond, cut short, the features of her face blurred in the vision state. She wore a gown the color of periwinkle.

Gorgeous. She was drop-dead gorgeous, whoever she was—and trouble, through and through.

The image of that enchanting faerie maiden vanished before I could figure out what it meant or what, if anything, it had to do with why my mother had brought me here.

In the image, I stood, under a night sky. The stench of ash filled the air.

"Weir," a voice whispered, in an accent that hinted at Ireland. Beautiful, but filled with pain. "You did everything you could do. Perhaps the Rose was right, and the stars—"

"Screw the stars," my vision-self whispered. "What if we've been making our own fates all along?"

A dark cloud swept over the water, like black ink pooled into a clear pool.

I was jerked out of the vision and into the present, like suddenly waking from a dream.

"What does it mean?" I gasped, throat aching, raw.

Who was the woman in my visions? What about the raven? And that last vision? Whose blood stained my clothing? And who was the Rose?

I turned to Mom. I didn't have to ask if she'd seen. I saw my own fear reflected in her own eyes. "I don't know. You know as well as I do, a seer's work is not to explain the vision." She reached up to cup my face. "You understand now what I've said for years."

I nodded. "The seer is not the scribe. Only the vessel."

For the first time, I did truly understand what she felt every time she had a vision. She couldn't control the outcome, only witness what was to come.

Her hand came to my face, soft, yet slightly rough with the familiar callouses earned through decades of hard labor.

"You can face what comes next, my little cub. We all can. Like your sister, embrace your magic. Deepen it. The witch and the shifter, both. That is the path forward."

Mom's eyes widened. "Weir, you have to go. There's something...Go. Now."

My vision shifted, shadows blurring out the cavern's dim light. Tingles erupted all over every inch of my skin.

I didn't even get a chance to say goodbye as the magic whisked me away, back to the one place I very much didn't want to be.

Chapter Three

Siobhan

"Do you really think this will work?" Vi asked, leaning close, her voice a hushed whisper.

I gave her a reassuring smile. Well, what I hoped was a reassuring smile. "I know it will."

I'd helped the coven create a ritual to access the key's magic based on the story of Biddy Marlowe. Even Nick seemed impressed by my knowledge of what Bailee called "the oral tradition," so I'd take that as a good sign.

Of course, with a healthy dose of my fae magic, I could easily part the veil between the human and faerie realms. But I couldn't tell the coven that—not without blowing my cover.

Still, now that we'd solved the riddlebound, the next part should be easy. Perform the ritual to find the location of the seven missing coven members and use the key to release them.

The tricky part would be doing all of that without revealing my true nature.

I shifted the wicker basket against my hip as we trudged through the woods. Cassie felt that performing the spell on the banks of Willow Creek would be best, since that's where the coven's energy was the strongest. We'd filled a few baskets and tote bags with the necessary items for the ritual and were making our way there now.

The early afternoon sun prickled against my skin, sending a trickle of sweat trailing down my spine. Truthfully, if I harnessed my full faerie ability, I wouldn't need all the crystals, herbs, books, and magical tools we carried with us. I could've performed the spell in a minute flat with nothing more than the key and the magic that sang in my veins.

But I couldn't exactly do that while I was pretending to be a witch. And no way the coven would let that key out of their sight.

So, here I was.

Evan jogged up the hill, joining me and Vi.

"So, Siobhan, what part of Ireland are you from?"

"County Clare. A tiny little village well off the beaten path."

"Kinda like an Irish version of Willow Creek?" he asked.

"Sort of. We have a pub a lot like Uncle Mick's place, some little shops, things like that." I didn't dare tell him that mere mortals rarely visited, that everyone there was full-blooded fae.

"These kinds of places have an appeal, don't they?"

"Yeah," I agreed. "Except everybody always knows your business, always meddling in your affairs."

He laughed. "You sound just like Nick. Although, look at him." He jutted his chin toward his brother, who walked hand in hand with Cassie, a basket tucked against one hip. Cassie had a tote bag slung over her arm, leaning close to Nick as he spoke.

A pang of jealousy filled my chest, but I tamped it down. No. No way anyone would ever look at me like that. Back home, I was Siobhan O'Shea, and *everybody* knew my destiny—the Rose had prophesied it before I was even born, after all.

And here?

Well, here in Willow Creek, I was a stranger. And worse than that, I was a fraud, living up to the fae reputation for trickery.

"You know, you might find that the small-town life grows on you," Evan said, giving me a charming grin and a conspiratorial wink. "I mean, Bailee loves it so much that she gave up life in the big-city."

Bailee, Evan's girlfriend, sidled up to him, a stack of books pressed against her chest. "What can I say? I always wanted to be a librarian at a small local library. And everything just sort of fell into place."

The lovey-dovey look she gave Evan told me that it wasn't just landing her dream job that made her want to settle in Willow Creek. Apparently, the two of them had been in love "since forever," as Nick put it, but only now were admitting they were a couple.

Add in Vi and her fox-shifter boyfriend, Aiden, and I was well beyond a third wheel in this little mystical adventure.

The sound of water cascading over stone met my ears, and the knots of tension forming in my shoulders and neck loosened.

We emerged on the banks of the creek, where clear waters played music as they danced along the earth and rock. Willow trees bowed their heads low, their weeping green branches reaching toward the water.

It was a picturesque spot for casting a spell, but the faerie in me could tell that the magic here was sick.

Some dark magic had been worked in this place, and it was siphoning away the mystical energy of Willow Creek.

This wasn't just any small town, and the Willow Creek Coven was only just beginning to realize that they weren't just any coven. Willow Creek was a nexus, a place where magic poured into this world from some place beyond this realm, beyond even the fae realms, where magic was pure and wild.

Witches had guarded the nexus for generations, with the help of a fae-appointed guardian. Now, the nexus might fall into the hand of a single half-fae man who wanted to use that power for himself.

With it, he could bring down anyone—even the most powerful of fae. Even entire faerie courts.

And in doing so, he would destroy this small town and everyone in it. Drawing that much power from a nexus came at a cost.

"Don't worry," Bailee said, settling her stack of books on a blanket that Cassie had spread out. She pushed her glasses back up her nose. "The spell will work. Between my research and your knowledge of the oral tradition, I'm sure we've got the right components."

I forced a laugh. "I guess it's true what they say. When in doubt, consult your local librarian."

"And if we don't know the answer, we know how to find it," Bailee finished. She cracked open a book, her finger sliding down a page of magical correspondences. "I want to double-check we've got the right crystals," she explained.

I nodded. The entire coven buzzed like a beehive, full of energy, everybody doing their part to make the ritual happen. Tapestry spread over rock. Candles, crystals, and herbs arranged in just the right way.

Unsure what to do, I slipped into the forest. Maidenhair ferns grew in the moist soil, and I knelt.

"Earth so sweet and wild, I come to you, your faerie child," I whispered, the earth beneath my palm buzzing with its soft electric energy. "May I take some of these precious ferns for my and my friends' altar?"

I waited. There was a heavy sigh, and then, "Take what ye will, and bring the lost ones back. The elementals have hidden themselves."

"I'll do everything in my power to see the elemental creatures return very soon," I whispered.

It was one-hundred precent the truth, a solemn promise I meant to keep.

Gently, I picked a few of the ferns, thanking the earth for this blessing as I returned.

Vi and Cassie were arranging the crystals on the altar.

"Here," I said, thrusting the ferns toward them, suddenly feeling like an interloper. I mean, I *was* an interloper, after all, wasn't I? "I thought we could add these to the altar. If that's okay."

"Of course," Cassie said. She stepped aside. "Feel free to place them wherever feels right to you. I think it's a good idea. Some earth magic, and something to connect the forests of Willow Creek to whatever place in the faerie realm we're trying to reach."

Careful to keep the crisp green fronds away from the candles, I added the ferns to the mixture of foxglove, marigolds, and rosemary on the altar, admiring the way it contrasted with the purple amethyst and labradorite crystals Bailee and Vi had chosen.

I toyed with the labradorite pendant that hung at my own neck. An oval stone set in swirls of silver filigree, it was a connection to both my family and my magic. *Remember that your gift is not a burden*, my aunt had whispered as she'd fastened the clasp around my neck when she gave it to me. My parents had chosen to go to one of the faerie realms when I was a child. Aunt Fiona had taken me in, raised me like one of her own daughters.

It sure feels like one, I'd quipped back.

Aiden came to kneel before the altar, adding a deer antler. "I found it on a hike in these woods years ago," he explained. "It feels like it belongs here."

I nodded. "It does."

I swallowed hard. I wished those who'd sent me could see this magic—its simplicity, its earnestness, how thoughtful and sincere the coven was in everything it did.

There is hope for Willow Creek without our interference. That's what I wanted to tell them. That prophecies be damned, the coven didn't need my help.

Cassie clapped her hands together lightly. "I think we're ready to begin," she said.

The knots of tension seized me again, one forming like a hard, tight coil in my gut.

I wanted to run, to turn back, to stop lying.

But that wasn't me. I never turned back. Not even when I should.

***

Weir

The ground beneath me was cold and hard. I stirred, desperately wishing I was back in the mystical cavern with my mom—or, even more, that I was back in Willow Creek, the entire family together again for Sunday dinner.

I blinked, the cave I'd taken shelter in coming into view.

I heard a growl, and then heavy breathing.

I wasn't alone.

"He stinks," a deep voice grumbled from the other side of a large cluster of tall rocks.

"Still, though...you think he's worth anything?" another voice rumbled back.

A scent tickled my nostrils, not at all pleasant—something like the world's worst BO.

Crap. That smell could only mean one thing.

Trolls.

I sprang to my feet, hood falling away from my face. I crept toward the rocks that separated me from the trolls. I needed to assess the situation.

Trolls. About six and a half feet tall, these guys looked like they were carved out of the gray rock that filled the cave. They were between me and the only entrance to the cave, meaning I was completely trapped.

As if on cue, two sets of beady black eyes stared at me with a mixture of malice and amusement that sent a shiver down my spine.

"How do you think it got in?" the first one said, cocking his head as he studied me.

His companion—the shorter of the two, but somehow with an even stockier build—shrugged. "Beats me. Found a doorway? That happens, right? Humans wander into the realm sometimes. Who cares?"

Okay. So my survival depended on not losing my cool, on keeping my wits about me. How did I play this? There were two of them, one of me, and they had me on both size and sheer muscle. I didn't see any weapons, but that didn't meant they weren't armed. Not that it mattered. They wouldn't need anything other than their fists to pummel me into dust.

How much magic did trolls have, exactly? My sister, Winnie, would've known. She was the one who loved folklore, especially anything to do with the fae and other magical beings.

Me? I favored my shifter ability over my witchcraft.

Could I shift? I'd avoided it because our high priestess, Ginny, had warned me that human shifter magic was sometimes unpredictable in the faerie realms. I could be unable to shift, or get stuck mid-shift, some sort of freaky half-human, half-puma creature. Or I could become trapped in my puma form for centuries.

"Does it talk?" the first one asked.

His companion turned to me. "Do. You. Talk?" He spoke slowly, grinding out the syllables.

Ye gods. They thought I was some hapless caveman, didn't they?

Good. Maybe I could use that to my advantage.

I stared at him blankly, trying to look as innocent as possible.

They exchanged a look. "Guess not," the one who'd addressed me said. "Do you suppose the Wise Woman would know what to do with it?"

His friend rolled his eyes. "We're not going all that way to find out what to do with some stray human. Maybe we just leave him where we found him."

"We could sell it. Market's not more than a two-day journey. Someone might want it as a servant or something."

Oh, crap. No way was I getting traded around by faeries like some sort of pet. For all I knew, I'd end up in a giant birdcage, hanging from the ceiling of some mountain troll's cavern.

I didn't have a choice. I had to shift. There was no time to disrobe either, and since my clothing wouldn't survive the shift, I'd either be stuck in my puma form for a while or I'd have to acquire new clothing before I could shift back. Not an easy thing to do when you're in animal form.

Goddess Artemis, goddess of the moon and wild things, guide me in my shift. Let the magic flow through me...

I didn't dare utter the incantation aloud, but I figured the magic would work just the same.

It had to.

Magic tingled against my skin. I let the cloak slide off, revealing the simple t-shirt and cargo pants I wore underneath. Those would vanish post-shift. Didn't matter.

Right now, evading capture by a couple of trolls was my number one priority. I could find new clothes later—preferably before frostbite got the better of me.

The magic began to hum.

"Hey—" one of the trolls said.

A gust of wind howled through the cave.

A burst of magic slammed into me, sending me flying into a rock wall.

I blinked, fighting to rise, stars dancing in my vision. The magic of my shift had sent us all flying, apparently—the trolls were still struggling to rise.

When I looked down, in place of human hands and feet I saw sandy-colored paws.

I guess shifting worked a bit differently in the faerie realms—but it still worked.

No time to stay and gloat, though. The trolls wouldn't be down for the count for long.

Time to do what I did best.

I ran.

Chapter Four

Siobhan

The key lay in the center of the altar, buzzing so loudly with faerie magic I almost had to cover my ears.

Okay, so maybe it wasn't so much a buzz as it was a siren's song of mystical energy.

But, as I watched Nick, Cassie, and the other coven members call the quarters and cast the sacred circle, I forced myself to stay still. I'd never really been the patient type, and watching them use witchcraft to do something in a matter of hours when I could've done it almost instantly with my faerie magic was definitely taxing.

But they couldn't know. Aunt Fiona assured me that witches wouldn't trust a full-blown faerie in their midst. And so, I waited.

Evan Felson stepped up to the altar and picked up a pentacle engraved on a piece of clay glazed the deep green of the ivy that climbed my cottage back home. "Guardians of the North and Elements of Earth, protect our sacred circle today. Keep it and all within safe. An it harm none, so mote it be."

Tingles of energy swept over me. The elementals of Willow Creek might've vanished, but the nexus still responded to the witches' magic.

Evan stepped back into the circle with the rest of us. We joined hands, crying, "Hand in hand, the circle is cast!"

The chant rose into the afternoon sky, like a bird on wing. My body grew lighter as the magic coursed through me, a smile flickering across my lips.

Faerie magic might be ancient, deep, and wild, but there was an earthy sweetness in witchcraft that had its own charm. That magic rippled through the air around us like a breeze.

Bailee stepped forward and lit a candle, a purple pillar engraved with a faerie star. The flame sputtered and then flared to life, a golden glow amid the backdrop of ferns, crystals, and other natural baubles we'd placed on the altar.

"We witches wise, we part the veil," she said, her voice solemn yet husky.

"We witches wise, we part the veil," we all chanted.

"Reunite us with what is lost," Nick called out, and we echoed his words.

"Open the door between the realms.

"Magic to magic we call to the other side.

"May stone be air and tree be wind.

"Unlock the door, and bring them home."

The flame flared, seeming to grow brighter with each line of the incantation. I could feel the magic building. Out of the corner of my eye, I caught a glimpse of something, a silvery light flickering around a deep blue door.

I turned, but just as quickly, the door vanished.

The ritual wasn't enough.

Ours was no simple task. We weren't just trying to cross over into one of the faerie realms. That was big magic, but manageable.

This? This was gigantic magic for witches. Objects made of faerie magic were often designed not to have witches meddle with them.

The key could unlock the door—but it needed faerie magic to do so.

My hands itched with pent-up magic, ready to be unleashed. I could grab the key, cross between the worlds, and find the missing coven members before those gathered here could finish their chant.

But in doing so, I'd reveal my true nature.

"Keep chanting," Cassie urged.

We repeated the incantation. The flame of the purple candle flickered, caught in the whirlwind of our spell. The sky darkened, a dense bank of fog sweeping over the creek's waters as the natural elements around us responded to powerful magic.

A metallic cling sounded in the air.

The key rose from its resting place on the stone altar.

"It's working!" Evan cried out.

"Keep going," Bailee urged.

The coven began to chant again.

The key spun in the air, but there was something off about its movement. It felt frenzied, its magic pulsating erratically.

"Open the door. Let us bring them home!" Bailee shouted.

No.

Too late I realized what was happening.

The key had a self-destruct. We'd managed to solve the riddlebound, but the fae who'd created it had put another layer of protection in place.

If anyone attempted to use the key with witchcraft, the key would destroy itself.

"We have to stop!" I cried out.

"No. Look," Vi said. "We're so close."

The key swirled in circles. But it wasn't about to unlock any door. It was about to vanish—and with it, our chance of rescuing the Willow Creek Coven would vanish too.

I couldn't let that happen. We couldn't come this close only to fail. And tomorrow night, I would need the coven's help to stop Weylin Felson from taking the nexus's magic for himself.

I released Vi and Evan's hands—each on either side of me. The key was a good ten feet in the air now, so there was only one way to reach it.

The coven kept chanting, everyone too swept in the magic.

"I'm sorry," I whispered, though no one heard.

They'd know soon enough that I'd lied to them. At least I wouldn't be around to see the looks on their faces when they discovered my betrayal.

In a powerful wave of faerie magic, I transformed, from woman to raven in mere seconds.

With a caw of warning, I flew toward the key. Waves of magic rippled through the air like gale-force winds, but I fought them off. I flew upward and then dove down.

I grabbed the key in my beak by its metal ring.

I had to get it away from the coven before their magic unknowingly destroyed the key.

So I flew higher and higher, above the trees.

I kept flying, not daring to look down, too afraid to look back.

The trees blurred into one giant green mass beneath me as I headed deeper into the mountains, toward Uncle Mick's cabin.

With any luck, he'd be able to smooth things over with the coven.

With even more luck, I could rescue the missing coven members and return them to Willow Creek before he could even finish explaining my side of things.

***

Weir

Run.

That single word thundered through my head, throbbing in my veins, thudded with every heartbeat as my paws hit icy stone.

I rounded the corner of the cave's entrance at full speed, my paws skidding against the packed snow. I slid into a jagged rock hard enough that there would surely be a bruise when I returned to my human form, but I didn't let it slow me down.

I was sandy fur, pure muscle, paws and sinew—and one-hundred-and-ten percent adrenaline. Escape was the only thing that mattered.

Somewhere behind me, a growl sounded, followed by a series of outraged cries, but I didn't take the time to turn around.

The Mountain Pass was narrow, without many places to hide—only the caverns that dotted this part of the treacherous pass.

Lost. In my human form, I'd been lost for weeks. All the mountains looked the same from this angle, rock and snow and peaks like the jagged teeth of some ancient, wintry dragon.

I skidded in the pack snow and ice as I rounded the next bend, narrowly catching myself from tumbling down a cliff.

Note to self: slow when rounding the curves so I didn't go careening off the edge into some endless abyss.

There were no villages, no quaint little inns or houses with smoke puffing from chimneys. Perhaps there were—in other, less brutal parts of the Winter Realm—but not here. Here, there was only the narrow pass, a series of blizzards and biting wind.

Endless winter. Endless foes. Endless threats.

An infinite number of ways to die.

My lungs ached, even in this form. Pumas were meant to run for short bursts chasing prey. They weren't meant to run for miles and miles. But I kept running anyway.

Surely those lumbering trolls weren't that fast. I slowed further, spots dancing in my vision.

Don't pass out now.

I found a trio of sharp, jagged rocks and slinked behind it. I let my animal body fall to the cold ground, the icy air burning with each breath.

With any luck, the trolls had lost interest in me. Maybe I'd been a mere curiosity, and they wouldn't bother to chase me very far.

I glanced up at the darkening sky, the clouds heavy and low, a dark and haunting blue that foretold of a deep snow to come.

With any luck? I snorted.

Luck?

No. Luck hadn't been on my side in a long, long time.

Chapter Five

Siobhan

Uncle Mick rubbed his temples. The man was notoriously even-tempered, but even I could sense that I'd irked him with the mess I'd made.

"Explain to me again, little bird," he said. "Why did you steal the key?"

"It was about to self-destruct."

"How, in the Rose's good name, could you tell?"

Uh-oh. He was taking the Rose's name in vain. Never a good sign. A fae ancient beyond measure, one of the few remaining earthbound fae who remembered when the worlds divided, our faerie family took her and her powers very seriously.

Not good, Siobhan.

"I just sensed it, okay?" I exhaled, turning away from my uncle toward the interior of the cabin, where oil paintings of mountains by a local artist decorated the wood walls. One wall was taken up entirely by musical instruments, everything from guitar to dulcimer to mandolin to fiddle hanging freshly polished, each instrument well-used and well-maintained.

I wish I'd come to Willow Creek just to listen to Uncle Mick play, and not to meddle in the affairs of witches.

"You could've been wrong. And even if you weren't, you had other options. You could've told the coven members that you suspected—"

"They wouldn't have listened!" I shouted, not bothering to wait for him to finish. "Look, I'm doing what I was sent here to

43

do. Don't get in a bluster with me because I did things on my own terms. You weren't there."

"No, I wasn't, but you've been training your whole life for this. You should've found a better way than plain ol' thievery in broad daylight in front of the whole coven. There's not enough smooth-talking in the world I can do to make this right."

I groaned, ready to rip my hair out. Instead, I grabbed the key off the table and glared at my uncle. "I never wanted this 'assignment.' I never wanted any of this."

"Siobhan," Uncle Mick said, his voice softening. "You're the one the prophecy spoke of. Since before you were born."

I blinked, all my rage fading at the kindness in his voice. But I wasn't comforted. "You know I would've rather it been anyone but me."

"I know, love," he said, the words like honey. "But you were chosen for this task for a reason. I don't have to tell you what the stakes are."

"We never should've lied. It was Aunt Fiona's idea, and a terrible one. I can't...Uncle Mick, I can't do this by committee anymore." I tucked the key into my pocket. "From here on out, I'm flying solo—literally and figuratively."

He stared at me for a long moment, then nodded. "I'll tell Fiona."

"Don't bother," I said. "The Rose will tell her soon enough."

Before he could try to talk some sense into me—or worse, get my bossy, meddling aunt on the line—I walked out the door and across the yard into the privacy of the woods.

Magic, on my own terms.

The hot sun, burning bright in a cloudless sky, threatened to sear my skin as I stomped off toward the woods. Maybe, when I returned with the missing coven members, I could explain *without* giving away my faerie identity. They said a member of their coven was half-witch, half-shifter. It was a rare combination—usually, a person inherited one type of magic or the other. The ability to cast spells as a witch, or the ability to transform into a particular animal as a shifter.

If a member of the Willow Creek Coven possessed such a one-in-a-million gift, perhaps, it wouldn't be so farfetched for them to believe I was one too. Both witch and shifter.

And not one-hundred-percent faerie.

I sighed.

I'd have to cross that bridge when I came to it. Because reuniting the coven with the seven missing witches was only step one in the plan I'd been given.

And the final step? My stomach churned as I thought about what the Rose expected me to do.

I knelt beneath the trees, tall ashes and oaks sheltering me in a forest full of birdsong and wild things. A rabbit skittered through the underbrush. I sensed a fawn's energy nearby, sleepy and sweet, resting tucked away with its mother somewhere close. A robin landed in the branches of the oak tree above me. I could feel her studying me.

She cocked her head, as if trying to figure out what I was.

When she sensed the raven within, she flew away.

I stared at the key resting in my hand, rotating it from one palm to the other.

After Bailee had risked her life to release the key from the riddlebound, I'd gone and stolen it. Mid-ritual.

"It doesn't matter," I whispered. The Rose would say the results mattered. But she hadn't interacted with humans in centuries, so maybe she wasn't the most reliable source on the subject.

Too late. Damage done.

I inhaled, clutching the key in one hand while with the other I pressed into the earth, drawing its energy into me. The earth's magic would stabilize and ground me while shoring up my own magic.

I came into a low lunge, one hand on the ground, the other holding the key.

"Take me to him," I growled.

Wait...him? No. To them. I'd meant to say them.

It didn't matter. The magic would work just as well.

The ground underneath me shifted, rippling with impending magic.

And then it was there again. The doorway, the same one I'd seen before. Wood painted the deepest blue, a tree made up of intricate Celtic knots painted on it in silver. Silvery-blue light pooled around its edge, and cold air wafted toward me like winter air seeping through a drafty door.

I stood.

It worked. The seven missing coven members should be waiting just on the other side of that door. And in my hand, I held the key to their prison.

I was so close.

I rose and tugged at the large silver ring on the door, hitting it with a dose of my faerie magic.

It swung open easily under my touch.

I couldn't see what lay beyond. I guess I'd just have to trust the magic that had brought the door to me. The air that wafted through was cold, speaking of winter, so I quickly wove myself a cloak out of faerie magic—something practical, a deep gray made of thick, sturdy fabric. I added matching boots to keep my feet warm.

And then, before the magic that summoned the door could dissipate, I stepped through.

***

Weir

My eyes flew open as a gust of cold air hit my body, a contrast to the cool but much warmer air of the cavern. Gray stone. White drifts of snow. The sky above that same endless bank of gray clouds.

I was still in my puma form, my sandy body a contrast to the white and gray. In a normal environment, it would be a sort of camouflage, but the color contrasted just enough with the snow and rock to be a dead giveaway in this icy realm.

I had to get out of here. I couldn't risk shifting back—in my puma form, I could tolerate the frigid temperatures much better than as a human. And, thanks to the lovely quirks of shifter magic, when I shifted back to human form, the mystical cloak and *every* shred of my clothing would be gone.

Great. Things had gone from bad to worse.

I rose, stretching before settling back on my haunches to examine my environment. I couldn't catch the scent of the trolls anywhere nearby, even though I was definitely downwind—and trolls had a very distinctive and unpleasant odor about them.

I was alone. A shiver rushed over me as I let that fact settle in.

I'd also left the cauldron, with its magical culinary offerings, behind in the cave where I'd encountered the trolls. And there were no smaller critters I could hunt for sustenance, whether as a puma or a man.

No shelter. No clothing. No food.

Surrounded by the unfriendliest of fae.

A doorway. Now more than ever, I needed a doorway out of this world.

I shivered again. Warmth. All I wanted was warmth. The puma in me wanted a great stretch of rock in the summer sun and a long nap. The man wanted blue sky, green trees, and a warm, homecooked meal beyond what the cauldron had produced.

Shepherd's pie, maybe.

Yes. I allowed myself to fantasize. A big slice of Dad's famous shepherd's pie, with a salad of greens freshly picked from the garden, and Mom's hot bacon dressing.

My stomach growled.

Apple pie a la mode. A cup of coffee.

My stomach growled again. I suppressed a whimper.

If the cold didn't get me, the hunger would for sure.

But I couldn't stay in one place. That was the way to certain death. I shook myself off and stepped out from behind the large stand of gray stone that concealed me. I scented the air again, listening carefully for the sounds of voices, footfalls, or any sign that someone was approaching.

Silence, except...

A raven's call. A tinkling of bells.

A scent wafted over me. Summer. A summer forest filled with ferns and rich earth.

Was I hallucinating? No. I was cold, but not that cold.

It wasn't my imagination. It was magic.

I inhaled again. Again, the scent of ferns and sunshine. I could almost feel the warmth.

I glanced around. Was someone nearby? Had I tapped into my own earth magic, as Mom had suggested?

No. Whatever it was, it wasn't coming from me.

The magic hit me full force, like a gust of wind from a coming storm. Hot, humid air whirled around me.

I wanted to bask in it, let it warm me inside and out, but then I saw the source: a doorway.

Deep blue like the color of twilight, it shimmered in a pool of silvery light.

My chance. Somehow, against all the odds, I'd found a doorway.

The door pull was silver, sparkling despite the cold, dull light of this place. I would have to shift in order to open the door.

I didn't even know where it led.

It didn't matter. This was my chance, and I was taking it.

I shifted in the space of three heartbeats. I gave a quick shout of thanks to the goddess, that my shifter magic had worked, that I wasn't stuck in my puma form. I was naked, but fully human.

Before the door could vanish, I ran, my bare feet burning in the snow as I rushed toward the waiting door.

I tugged on the silver ring and the door swung open, offering me a pool of waiting green light to step into.

Imagining a summer sky, I stepped through.

Part Two: The Summer Realm

"I met a lady in the meads,
Full beautiful—a faery's child,
Her hair was long, her foot was light,
And her eyes were wild."
—John Keats, "La Belle Dame Sans Merci"

Chapter Six

Siobhan

Something hit me with a crash.

Usually the pathway between worlds was soft and smooth, a pool of glittering light that shivered across my skin like a waterfall's mist. But this time, I hit something heavy.

No, not something. *Someone.*

They gave a slight 'oof' sound as we collided.

In a vibrant flash of green light, we crashed to the ground, a tangle of limbs.

"Ow," a male voice grumbled.

As soon as I hit, I forced myself into a roll, moving away from my would-be attacker. I quickly brought myself into a lunge, grateful that my extensive training included some basic combat skills.

I blinked, taking in my potential opponent and our surroundings.

The man lay on the ground, seeming a bit out of it. And also—naked. Like, completely bare-ass naked.

He sat up, rubbing his head, and looked at me. He was gorgeous, the man who'd nearly landed on top of me. Chestnut hair, mussed from our fall, framed a face with chiseled features and an olive complexion.

"Hi?" he said, looking all sorts of confused.

"Hi?" I repeated, narrowing my gaze. As I did, the raven in me sensed something—an animal of some kind in him. "You're a shifter."

"Yeah." He ran his fingers through his hair, that deep gray gaze sliding over me. "Uh, post-shift, obviously. But I didn't want to miss the doorway before it closed."

"The doorway!" I jumped up, staring at the place where the doorway had been only seconds earlier. "Shit!"

I turned to glare at him. "That was my doorway," I growled. "What the hell were you doing leaping into it?"

He stood, then seemed to remember his conspicuous lack of clothing and turned away from me so I could only see his side profile.

"I was trying to get home," he said.

"What made you think *my* doorway, that I summoned, with *my* magic, would take you home?"

"Look, I'm not an expert in magical doorways, okay. I was lost in the Winter Realm, quite literally freezing my ass off, and I saw a doorway. So I shifted back to my human form and I jumped through. I didn't realize it was *your* doorway," he said, glaring down at me as he said this last part.

I turned away, not wanting to admit that his nakedness was making me uncomfortable. I knew human witches were used to being naked in front of one another, but the truth was, I hadn't spent much time outside of my tight-knit faerie community. And this man's beautifully muscled form was making me feel all squirmy.

At twenty-two, I was an adult. A man, naked or not, shouldn't make me nervous. But this one was.

"Well, hurry up and conjure yourself some clothes," I said, gesturing at him as I turned away. "We have to summon another doorway."

"I can't conjure myself some clothes."

Unable to bring myself to look back at him, I exhaled and gazed skyward. Above us, a verdant canopy of large green leaves shielded us from the sun, the trees at least a hundred feet tall. The air smelled of ferns and mushrooms, of rich earth and wild things.

The Summer Realm. Not at all where I'd intended to end up.

"What were you thinking about when you entered the doorway?" I asked, rubbing my temples, a headache rapidly forming.

"Being warm again. Blue skies and all that jazz."

"I was afraid of that," I grumbled.

"Why? What happened?"

"I think our magicks sort of...collided. I summoned the doorway, and we both stepped through on opposite sides and now we're..." Wait. Had he said he couldn't conjure himself any clothes? Why not? That was some basic-level faerie magic. "You're human."

I couldn't prevent my gaze from flickering back to him, or catching that sheepish and charming grin that lit up his stubbled face. "Guilty as charged. What did you expect?"

"I mean..." I trailed off, trying to put the pieces together, but thoroughly rattled by everything. "What was a human shifter doing in the Winter Realm of the fae?"

"Trying to get *out* of the Winter Realm of the fae," he grumbled. "Which is where you were trying to go, judging by your outfit."

"Yes." Right, my outfit. I took off the cloak. I wouldn't need it in this realm of endless warmth. I held it out to the naked shifter in front of me. "Here. Put this on until we can find you something more...suitable."

He cleared his throat and turned away from me. When he turned back, he'd wrapped the cloak around his waist.

I grinned. "Nice look. Very stylish."

"Do you want me to be naked again?" he asked, quirking an eyebrow in challenge.

"No. Absolutely not." Heat filled my cheeks as I turned a no-doubt lovely shade of crimson.

"Okay, then." He glanced at the forest around us and whistled. "Whew. It's gorgeous here. Wherever here is."

"We're in the Summer Realm," I supplied.

"It's nice. Still not Willow Creek, but better than the last place I was."

My jaw fell open. Did he really just say...

"Willow Creek?" I repeated.

Was I hallucinating?

"Yeah." He stopped adjusting the cloak around his waist and glanced at me. "You've heard of it?"

"Yes, I have." The words came out breathless. The doorway had brought me closer than I thought. "But where are the others? The rest of the coven?"

"We were separated. They sent me to get help. Only I wasn't doing such a good job of it. When I saw the doorway, it felt like a dream come true. I had been wandering that pass for who knows how long, had a run-in with some trolls, shifted into my puma form and run for my life..."

I stepped toward him, examining his face closer for the first time. The angular lines of his jaw, his aquiline nose, those intense eyes shaded by thick lashes. "You're Weir, aren't you? Weir Delaney?"

"I am. Who are you?"

"Siobhan O'Shea. The coven..." I didn't want to lie, and they hadn't exactly sent me, had they? "I was on a mission to rescue the Willow Creek Coven when we collided."

"All by yourself? That's bold."

"No less bold than a human man wandering through the Mountain Pass. I guess no one told you that you need fae magic to get in and out of the pass."

"That explains why I felt like I was going in circles."

"Well, we have to go back," I said, brushing my hair away from my face.

"So, you have fae magic?"

I swallowed. I wasn't ready to blow my cover, not yet, so I'd best stick to my cover story. "Some. I'm witch and a shifter, like you. But I have a bit of faerie magic."

"Okay. Well, we just need another doorway. And maybe some better clothes for me. And then we rescue my mom and sis and the rest of the coven." He narrowed his gaze, the glint of his eyes hard as the edge of a shard of shale. "What exactly is your plan? How are you going to rescue them when no one else has been able to all this time?"

"I have a key," I said.

The realization hit me all at once, hard enough that I stumbled backward, coming to rest on the trunk of a fallen tree. "The key. It was in my hand when we...collided." I stood, panic rising in me.

"Okay," Weir said. "Look, it's got to be around here somewhere. Let's start looking."

Not exactly an easy task. Tall stands of ferns that came to my waist surrounded us, with ivy and clumps of bluebells growing underneath.

But what choice did we have?

Weir knelt on the forest floor and began combing through the dense vegetation. I tried not to study the curve of his backside or the lean muscles of his arms.

Instead, I knelt and began looking too.

The sooner we got out of the Summer Realm, the better—for more reasons than I could list. Not least of which was the fact that the Summer Queen was notoriously unwelcoming to the earthbound fae. Technically, I needed special permission to be here.

But I wasn't about to tell Weir that. Not unless I had to.

***

Weir

My would-be rescuer grumbled to herself as we searched for the key. She was, uh, wound a bit tight, to say the least.

But I guess I would be too if I was a one-woman rescue team for a coven of lost witches.

She could also very well be the woman from my vision. As soon as her scent washed over me—a scent of rain and oakmoss, of wild geraniums and some wild, unnamable flower—I'd suspected. Even before I'd seen her face.

Okay, so she wasn't wearing a dress the color of periwinkle and standing in some ancient fae temple. And her face in my vision hadn't exactly been crystal clear.

As a shifter, nakedness was a norm for me, and shifters saw one another naked all the time. But in this moment, I was very aware of my state of near-nakedness—and I regretted meeting Siobhan that way. She'd obviously been uncomfortable with it.

"I'm sorry I ruined your spell," I said, glancing over at her.

She exhaled and mumbled something in a language I didn't understand—Gaelic, maybe? "It's fine. Just keep looking for the key."

"I'm no expert at women, but I'm pretty sure 'it's fine' is code for 'it's really, really not fine,'" I said, attempting to lighten the mood—and maybe really wanting a smile out of my new-found companion.

She glared at me from a stand of ferns. "No, okay, it's not. Nothing has gone right this whole time, and this just..." She tossed her hands up in the air, gesturing broadly at the world around us.

I approached her, kneeling beside her, careful to readjust the cloak she'd given me. "I truly am sorry."

She nodded, meeting my gaze as she pushed her hair away from her face. "You don't have to be. If I'd been wandering the Mountain Pass, I would've jumped through the first doorway I saw too."

I glanced around at our surroundings. Tall trees stretched toward the sky, and birdsong filled the downright balmy air. In the distance, I heard the sound of rushing water—a stream, maybe? "At least we're in a relatively safe place."

She smiled ruefully. "Oh, you haven't met the summer fae."

"Should I be worried?" I countered.

"Depends on who we run into."

I nodded, swallowing hard. Of course, just because the weather in the Summer Realm was more hospitable, didn't mean realm's inhabitants would be. "Right. I guess we'd better find that key then, huh?"

She nodded, and we went back to work in silence, carefully turning back leaf, stem, and flower searching for the missing key.

"I have a hard time believing that, you know," she said after a few minutes of unproductive searching.

"Believing what?" I said, rummaging around under a large fern and coming up with nothing but a random piece of rough stone.

"That you aren't an expert at women. You seem like..." She trailed off. "Like the kind of man who's dated plenty."

I shrugged. "I was talking more about long-term relationships." I rolled the stone in my palm, its sandstone surface pleasantly rough against my palm.

"Oh," she said, her tone quiet, as if she were mulling that over.

I didn't expand on my answer. What would I say? That no one ever felt right? That my mom, the seer, told me when I was sixteen that, while not everyone has a destined mate, I did? That my sister told me she could always tell when a woman I was dating 'wasn't the one.'

You don't love her, Weir. It's obvious, she'd said when she'd met my last girlfriend. Her tone was matter-of-fact but not unkind.

Yeah. Living with an empath and a seer had its downsides.

I studied Siobhan as she searched, her eyes narrow, her mouth set in a scowl. Her hair and build were similar to the woman in the vision, but I couldn't be sure.

I shook my head, trying to clear my mind of the images floating through it. Maybe it had been too long since I'd met someone who didn't want to kill me—or who, at least, wasn't actively trying to kill me.

After thirty minutes of searching, shadows of descending twilight began to creep over the forest.

Siobhan gave a heavy sigh and slumped onto the fallen tree that crossed through the endless expanse of ferns, ivy, and flowers. "We're not going to find it."

I didn't want to admit it—not out loud, anyway—but I was starting to suspect you were right. I came to sit beside her, settling the cloak over my legs. "It means a lot to you, doesn't it? Rescuing the coven, I mean."

She shrugged and gazed up at the darkening sky. "It's been my destiny since before I was born."

"Huh."

An owl hooted in the distance. *Hoo-hoot-hoo-hoo. Hoo-hoot-hoo-hoo-oo.* I listened, the familiar sound oddly comforting in such a strange place. I'd spent plenty of nights on the back porch of our old farmhouse, listening to the cries of owls.

"Rescuing us has been your destiny before we even needed to be rescued?" I pressed her.

She gave me a sideways, you-can't-be-serious glance. "There's this...woman...where I'm from. A powerful seer. And she saw what would happen in Willow Creek. That the coven would be separated—some members in Willow Creek, some trapped in the faerie realm. And this seer saw that I would play a role in their rescue. Everyone back in my village knows who I am, what I'm destined for. And no one has ever, for a single second, let me forget it."

"I understand that part. My mom is a seer. My sister is an empath. They try to stay out of my business, but sometimes..."

"Sometimes?" she prodded.

"I don't have the same gifts they do. But I know when they know something. I know when they're hiding something, not telling me because they don't want me to feel the weight of what they know. And so I started asking them to tell me when it affected me directly. And I mostly wish I hadn't."

"Ah." She nodded, and it wasn't an empty gesture. Siobhan understood.

I stood and offered her my hand. "Why don't we find a place to sleep for the night? We'll hunt for the key again in the daylight."

"Oh, I'm fine to stay right here. You get some rest. I'll take first watch."

I smirked. "Roughing it in a faerie glen? Okay then."

"Oh, sorry. Did you want a quaint little bed-and-breakfast, then? Something charming, perhaps run by gnomes?"

"That depends. How many stars? Continental breakfast? Free wifi?"

Siobhan rolled her eyes. "Oh, yeah. Easy to come by all that in the Summer Realm."

She jutted her chin toward the ground. "Sleep. I'll wake you when it's your turn to be lookout."

"What if I'm not tired yet?" I stretched my legs out in front of me, gazing up at the canopy. Night was falling swiftly, its descent no doubt hastened by the thick canopy of the trees.

If Siobhan wanted company, someone to wile away the hours talking, she didn't show it. She shrugged again.

"Try counting sheep."

I cleared my throat. "Well, then. I guess it's goodnight."

Chapter Seven

Siobhan

The puma shifter snored—probably because this was the first time in a long while that he'd had a decent night's rest, judging by how deeply he slept.

He was sprawled on the forest floor, my cloak draped over his lanky body, his snore a deep, reverberating sound over a backdrop of night insects and owl's cries.

He might've slept, but I could not. Fortunately, my faerie eyesight allowed me better night vision than a human would have.

I couldn't shake the coil of dread that formed in my stomach. I'd messed up everything. I didn't know how or where, exactly, my mission had started to unravel—only that every step I took seemed to move me further away from the carefully crafted plan Aunt Fiona had spent more than two decades creating, the Rose guiding her every move.

I was alone now, without their guidance. I'd spent my entire life training, scarcely leaving our village except for once a year, when my Aunt Fiona and older cousins would take me to one of the human villages for a long weekend for a taste of how humans lived. My cousin Sinead had put together my outfits for my trip to America, crafting a style she said would suit "my persona," as she put it.

If everyone else had planned this mission, this quest down to the letter, then anything that went wrong was surely on me. In a few months, on Samhain, I would turn twenty-three. By then, according to the plan, I should be back on Irish soil, Willow Creek fast fading into a distant memory.

If everything went according to plan, in a few days, I would be free. My destiny would've played out. The prophecy would've come and gone. And then, my life would be my own.

The air was heavy with the scents of summer—the heady scent of flowers, many of which only grew in this realm, melded with the scent of ferns and pollen, a hint of mushrooms, everything dew-kissed and wild. And along with those scents, magic hummed in the air, a faint electric current of mystic energy that zipped along my skin.

In the morning, we'd find the key. I had to hope it hadn't tumbled out of my hand and into some other realm, that it was here, hidden somewhere in the dense vegetation.

If this had been the human realm, I could've sensed the key's faerie magic. But the magic here was simply too thick in the air, and it was impossible to separate out the key's magical hum from the rest of the fae magic around me.

I leaned against the log, blinking my heavy eyes. The darkness that had settled in, along with the warm-but-not-too-warm air made me long for sleep. I could just imagine curling up beside Weir, sleeping until the tendrils of dawn sunshine awakened us.

No. I forced my eyes open. I couldn't sleep. And this was probably the most rest Weir had gotten in ages. I couldn't bring myself to wake him so he could take a turn guarding.

An owl hooted somewhere nearby.

I didn't even hear the branches rustle as the creature took flight, but she must've. Because there she was—a small, brownish owl, gazing up at me from the log beside me, her eyes wide and blinking, dark pools flecked with magic.

"You're her familiar, aren't you?" I whispered. A quick glance at Weir assured me he still slept, curled up peacefully as a fawn on the forest floor.

The owl studied me, but I felt it. She was the Guardian's familiar—the Guardian, who watched over the Crossroads of Magic in Willow Creek. Or, who *had* watched over it, until Weylin Felson decided to claim it for himself.

"Does she live?" I whispered.

The owl stared up at me, and though she couldn't speak, I knew the answer.

My mistress clings to life. But soon she will be gone, and without another, the Crossroads of Magic will fall to him.

I nodded, holding my hand out to brush my fingertips lightly against her feathers. The owl was flesh and blood, but she was also magic and prophecy, a creature who could move between the worlds without needing a doorway. Such was her nature.

"I'll do my best not to fail you."

Feather and fae magic, came the soft, husky voice. *We are not so different. Each on a quest not of our choosing. When the dawn rises, the key will gleam in its light. You'll see, little raven.*

Then, without another sound, she took flight.

I didn't hear her cry again the rest of the night. I knew she'd vanished from this realm and into another, with a few gentle flaps of her wings.

Just before the dawn rose, I wove a bit of magic so Weir and I could begin our journey. I walked away, toward the banks of a nearby stream, and, in a soft glow of purple light, conjured a breakfast of fruit and soda bread, a canteen of fresh water, and a simple set of clothing for him. Hopefully he wouldn't ask too many questions about how I'd acquired these things. Conjuring was fae magic, after all—and as far as Weir knew, I was a witch-shifter, like him.

I stepped back into the ferny glade and set the items on the log, plopping a plump blackberry in my mouth and washing it down with a few sips of water.

Finally, I didn't think we could wait any longer. Dawn was almost here.

Soon I would know whether the Guardian's familiar had been right.

***

Weir

I woke to the sound of a melodic voice calling my name. She wrapped it in an accent that hinted at Ireland, a voice sweet and wild.

"Weir?" the voice called again.

"Mmmm," I said, rolling over and reaching toward that voice.

"Weir!" the voice whisper-shouted, a foot hitting me in the shin. "Wake up. I found us some breakfast—and some more appropriate clothing for you."

Her irritation should've burst the spell of slumbery pleasure like a soap bubble, but I just grinned and leaned back against the earth.

"Sounds good," I said, bringing my hands to rest underneath my head. Above us, the sky was deep blue, just hinting at the day to come.

"Gods." I couldn't see, but I swore I *felt* her roll her eyes at me. "We're on a rescue mission, not a holiday."

Reality came crashing back. Mom. Winnie. The rest of the coven.

I bolted upright, now fully awake.

Her hand came to my chest. "Calm down. I have a plan. Just get dressed and eat something before the sun rises."

I sucked in a deep breath. The air was cool and fresh, scented sweetly with forest and dew. "Okay. Right."

She thrust a stack of clothes into my hands, and I went behind a tree to tug them on. The memory of her hand against my chest remained, and I couldn't help but let my own linger there, where a heat remained seared in my skin.

The vision. I didn't know why I'd seen her. I couldn't be one-hundred-percent certain who the woman was, and yet I suspected it had been Siobhan. When I'd seen her, I'd felt this same heat, but also something that went far beyond it.

It didn't matter how I felt. All that mattered was that soon, Mom and Winnie would be safe back in Willow Creek, Winnie in front of her computer, gaming her heart out to her favorite MMORPG, and Mom at hers, clucking her tongue as she balanced the books or sent out invoices for the farrier business.

And Dad? Goddess, but he must've been worried sick.

I tugged the tunic shirt over my head. The pants were tight-fitting britches, the cloth snug but surprisingly soft. They appeared, in the dim light, a deep shade of blue, and the tunic was white with some sort of silver thread.

I no doubt looked Renaissance-Faire ready, but I doubted they sold t-shirts and cargo shorts in the Summer Realm, and something was better than nothing.

I re-emerged, and Siobhan immediately thrust a canteen at me. I chugged a few long, deep sips of water.

"So, tell me this plan of yours?" I said, taking the food she offered me.

I tore off a large chunk of bread, my stomach grumbling at the mere sight of it. I was going to need something more substantial than bread and berries before long.

"We had a little visit last night during your snore-fest. The Guardian's familiar stopped by."

"The. Guardian's? Familiar? Okay?" I tried to pretend that I knew what she was talking about, but I'd paid far more attention to shifter lore over the years than other types of magical lore.

"The Guardian of the Crossroads of magic. Her companion—the owl. And let's just say she told me that today, when the sun rises, the key will reveal itself somehow and we'll be able to find it and get on our merry well. We grab the key, open a door to the Winter Realm, and we're all back in Willow Creek in time for happy hour at the Thirsty Fiddler."

"You think it will be that simple? Because the coven and I tried for months to bust our way out of that place."

"You didn't have the key then. We will. Fae magic is a tough thing to break. Any kind of fae enchantment will beat witchy magic any time. But this time, we'll have a key enchanted with faerie magic, so we're golden."

"And what about Weylin? What if we run into him?"

A dark expression skittered across her face, like a cloud briefly blotting out the full moon's light. But then she shrugged. "No reason to think we will. He's probably preparing for the big battle that everyone keeps prophesizing..."

"Wait." I raked a hand through my hair, exhaling slowly, trying to steady myself. "What battle?"

She frowned, the consternation on her face visible even in the dim light. "You don't know?"

"Obviously not."

"On the night of the black moon—that's tomorrow—there will be a battle between the witches of Willow Creek and Weylin Felson for control of the Crossroads of Magic."

"And if we lose, he gains control?"

"You won't lose," she said simply. "You—we—can't lose."

"Why not?"

"There's too much at stake."

"Such as?" I pressed. Mom had said the same thing. *Ruin.*

Siobhan didn't answer, though. Instead, she turned away and glanced up at the sky. "The sun will rise in just a few minutes. Be on the lookout for the key."

There was something off about Siobhan O'Shea. She was evasive at just the right—or, perhaps, wrong—moments. It didn't take magic to figure out she was hiding something.

Was it something she knew or something she was doing? Was she merely withholding unpleasant information—or was she up to something? It felt like the first, but I couldn't be sure.

"Almost," she whispered, her gaze fixated on the skyline, where hints of growing light began to appear. "We'll only have a minute, so be ready."

"I'm ready," I assured her. Whether or not Siobhan was hiding something, she was my best chance to free the coven—and probably my only chance of getting out of the Summer Realm and back to Willow Creek.

The horizon glowed with the promise of morning sunshine. Any second now.

And then I heard it.

"Siobhan." I grabbed her wrist.

"What?" she hissed.

"I hear..."

What was that? Could it be?

Her hand sought mine in the not-quite-darkness.

Hooves beating against firm earth announced the arrival of a visitor. No, more than one. At least two, by the sounds of it.

We weren't alone in our secluded little glade anymore.

Chapter Eight

Siobhan

I gripped Weir's hand.

I didn't know why—I wasn't exactly the hand-clutching type, after all. Way too damsel in distress for my taste.

Just stay out of Asteria's realm, my dear, Aunt Fiona had told me when I was thirteen, when my tutor was teaching me about the realms of the fae. *She and the Rose have a complicated history. Asteria took it personally when the Rose stayed behind to lead the earthbound fae. We can't go there without permission.*

And even though centuries had passed since that perceived slight? It wouldn't matter to the faerie queen. Weir and I were trespassers in her realm.

I squeezed Weir's hand more tightly. I hadn't known him even a day, but he was charming, smart, a little snarky. Hot? Yeah, that too.

And if I lost one of the humans I'd been sent to rescue from one faerie to another one? I couldn't live with that. I'd made enough mistakes in the past twenty-four hours, after all.

But maybe the key would reveal itself. I could open a door within seconds. And we could be gone before the approaching fae could do anything to stop us.

The sky grew lighter, bit by bit, until finally, a golden light infused the forest.

Dawn in an enchanted faerie forest was a sight to behold. Every leaf seemed to shiver, glistening with dew as they shook themselves awake. The flowers tilted their sleepy heads toward the sun, and a golden glow kissed the forest awake, breaking the spell of night with a kiss of sunshine.

The light swept over us.

"Look for the key," I whispered to Weir, forcing myself to drop his hand. "It will be glowing—literally glowing—in the dawn's light." At least, that was how I'd interpreted the owl's message.

He nodded. We searched in silence, a sense of urgency as we rustled ferns and searched the nooks of tree roots, looking for any sign of the key.

"Uh, Siobhan?"

"Yeah?" I said absently, continuing to scour the landscape for the magical key that would unlock the coven's prison.

"I know why we didn't find it last night. Look."

I turned toward him. He was pointing up.

I followed his gaze. The key. There, high in the tree canopy, the key and its accompanying gemstones glistened in a golden-green aura of light.

"How are we going to get it?" Weir asked.

"I have a way. I told you I was a shifter. Well, my animal form is a raven," I told him. Problem was, if he saw me shift back fully clothed, he'd know I wasn't a witch. "Stay hidden until I've got the key. Then, we'll open the door and make a break for it." He stared at me like I'd lost my mind. "I've got this," I insisted. "Hide. Now."

I waited until he was safely ensconced beneath the fallen log, his tall form tucked away behind tall stands of ferns and bluebells. And then I let the shift sweep over me, a swift wave of electrifying magic that transformed me from woman to raven in the blink of an eye.

In the fae realm and in my animal form, everything was heightened. The magic that hung in the air caressed my feathers like ribbons of silk.

But I didn't have time to bask in the sensation. I had to grab the key and transform back in time to create a doorway into the Winter Realm before we got caught. Our fae visitors were about to stumble upon our quaint little hiding place.

With a flap of my midnight wings, I took flight, launching myself into the tree canopy. I didn't have the swift, swooping motions of a barn swallow or the flitting, darting buzz of a hummingbird, but I still loved my raven form.

I flew closer and closer to the key, where it glimmered golden in the dawn's light.

So. Close.

In mid-flight, I grabbed for it with my beak.

And missed.

I circled back and prepared for a second try.

This time, my beak grasped the gold ring, the key dangling triumphantly from my beak.

"There! Look! I told you," a haughty voice sneered. "I'd bet the queen's crown that's no raven."

"No," his companion said, her voice a dry, husky tone. "But there's something un-fae going on here."

I landed, crouching down by the log and transforming, clothes and all. Pressing my palm against the earth, I called the magic to open the door. With this much fae magic and earth magic all around me, it would be nearly effortless.

The doorway began to sparkle, its silvery blue light appearing just feet from where we hid.

"Get ready to run," I whispered to Weir.

"Stop," the female voice growled. "Unless you want an arrow in your back faster than you can blink."

I turned away from the door, the magic dissipating.

An elven woman with short platinum hair and pointed ears sat atop a white horse, glaring down at me. She sneered. "Stand up," she commanded.

Hastily, I shoved the key in my front pocket, hoping she wouldn't notice. And then, I obeyed her command.

She sniffed, spearing me with a gaze as sharp as broken glass. Her eyes were green like peridot, but without a hint of mirth. She wore the garb of a warrior—an arrow already nocked in her bow, a quiver on her back, and a silver dagger strapped to her side. She rode bareback and sat straight and strong atop her horse.

Oh, no. A glance at her companion, clad in the same garb of gold and emerald green, told me exactly who they were.

Weir and I were face to face with two members of the Summer Queen's Guard.

***

Weir

Out of the frying pan and into the fire. It was one of Mom's favorite sayings—and far too appropriate for my current situation.

A woman who I could only imagine was an elf sat tall astride a horse whose coat shimmered like white silk covered in flecks of silver.

I stood on trembling legs and forced myself to meet her gaze. She cupped my chin, her sharp nails digging into my skin. She turned my head from one side then the other.

"This one's human," she said with a sneer.

Her companion—more squat and stocky than she was, his skin a greenish brown hue, chuckled. It was *not* a pleasant sound. I took an involuntary step back.

"Let's kill 'em here," he said, drawing a short sword from a scabbard with a metallic clang.

I shot a sideways glance at Siobhan. Her nostrils flared, and the hard set of her lips and jaw indicated more anger than fear, but she seemed like she might be the type who was good at hiding her true emotions.

"I wouldn't do that if I were you," Siobhan said, glowering at the fae man. "We're on very important business—business that Queen Asteria herself might want to know about."

The elven woman's eyebrows shot up in a sharp, quick V before her expression again became neutral. "I sincerely doubt that."

"How do you know the queen's name, trespasser?" the green man said. "You reek of the human world."

Siobhan tilted her chin up to meet him, her gaze defiant. Either her confidence would save us or get us both killed. But she seemed to have a plan, whereas I did not.

Questions swirled in my head. How did she conjure the doorway so quickly? How had she done shifted so quickly without disrobing?

And where had she *acquired* the clothes I wore?

This one's human. That was what the elven woman had said. About me. She'd said nothing about Siobhan. And Siobhan knew the name of the queen of the summer court.

"I have studied the lore of the faerie realms since I was a mere child. I know the queen's name. And you can tell her that Siobhan of the earthbound fae is here, and that she's on a mission from the Rose."

"She speaks nonsense," the greenish man said. "Shall I cut off her tongue?"

The elven woman glared down at Siobhan, her expression inscrutable. After a few long seconds, she held up a hand to her companion. "No. If she is who she claims, Queen Asteria will want to see her. And if she speaks lies, then the queen herself can determine both their fates."

A shiver slid down my spine. The Summer Realm might be far warmer and far more beautiful than the Mountain Pass of the Winter Realm, but it was proving to be equally as dangerous.

And Siobhan O'Shea, the Irish witch?

She obviously had more than her share of secrets—and maybe everything she'd told me was a lie, for that matter.

Siobhan met my eyes and gave me a quick shake of her head, as if to say she knew I had questions, but now wasn't the time.

"Walk ahead of the horses. If you try to run or work any magic, you'll regret it," the elven woman said. "If you've studied the realms as thoroughly as you claim, obviously you know what an elven curse can do to you."

Siobhan met my gaze. "I do," she said to the elven woman, her eyes telling me that such a fate wasn't one we dare tempt.

What choice did we have?

Silently, we walked through a gorgeous forest filled with trees that seemed thousands of years old, green and silver moss dripping from high branches.

I swallowed hard, keeping my eyes on the path ahead while never forgetting the arrow that was surely pointed at my back.

Chapter Nine

Siobhan

We walked—in silence broken only by the fae man's occasional off-key singing and the elven woman's snappish demands that he stop—for over an hour before we reached the Dale.

The capital city of the Summer Realm gleamed in shades of opulent gold mixed with every shade of green imaginable. The buildings were clad in brown stone flecked with gold, the roofs flat with rooftop gardens and suspension bridges that allowed the fae inhabitants to walk without ever touching the ground. The streets were a spiral shape with the queen's castle at the center, a tall building with spires reaching toward the blue sky, the stone nearly obscured by the flowers and vines that climbed ever upward.

And behind it all was a waterfall that flowed to the Lake of the Ages, a place of fae legend, its waters imbued with ancient powers so sacred that to take a single sip or collect a single drop without the queen's permission was punishable by death.

Weir leaned toward me. "Hot damn," he whispered.

Despite our plight, I couldn't the flicker of a smile that crossed my lips when I saw the way his eyes lit up.

"Impressive, isn't?" I said.

"It's...unimaginable. Look, there are barrels to catch the rainwater and..."

"Quiet," the elven woman hissed.

I held my head high as we passed through the streets of the Dale. Plenty of eyes spied us, but no one stopped us, spoke to us, or even came too close—that was the power of the queen's guard.

If we thought they were going to walk us through the grand halls of that shimmering castle, we were mistaken. Our captors dismounted their horses, leaving them in the care of a servant, and led us to a tunnel, where other members of the guard let us pass with a mere nod and a curious glance. The air in the tunnel was dank and musty, almost enough to make me forget about the golden sunlight glistening off rooftop gardens, or the roses in every hue that bloomed through the city.

We stopped in front of a large wooden door fitted with a small metal grate.

"Welcome to your new home," the greenish man said with a chuckle as he unlocked it. The door groaned heavily as he opened it. "Enjoy the accommodations."

"You can't be serious," Weir said.

"Weir..." I said in a warning tone.

"No. I didn't escape that tower and wander through the Winter Realm to be thrown into a literal dungeon."

"Unless you want a dagger in your belly, I'd do as you're told," the man growled.

Ah. I saw now why he was a member of the guard. Maybe not super-bright, but definitely mean—and apparently not squeamish.

"Weir," I said, keeping my voice calm, though inside I was pure jelly. "I'm sure this is just temporary until they can arrange a meeting with Queen Asteria."

The fae man threw back his head and guffawed. "Yeah, right. An audience with the queen."

The elven woman shot him a sharp look that silenced him. "Why don't you see that the stable hands have watered the horses?"

"I'm sure the boys can handle it."

"All the same," she said, in a tone that brooked no argument. It was clear that she held superior rank.

"Well, guess I'll get right on that."

Leaving the key dangling from the door handle, he sauntered off, his whistle echoing eerily back to us as he walked down the tunnel.

After his whistling and footsteps were long passed, the elven woman set her gaze on me.

"Siobhan O'Shea, of the earthbound fae? And this one is..." She peered at Weir. "Not fae, obviously. Witch. And something else?"

"Half-witch, half-shifter," I supplied. No use hiding it. She'd figure that part out soon enough. "And our mission is, well, time sensitive."

She smirked—ever-so-slightly. "If you are who I think you are, I'd say so. But you don't want the likes of that one knowing too much of your business. Quite the mouth on him. A few pints of ale at the local pub and he'd spill your secrets to the entire city before the night was over." She tugged the key from the lock and slid it into her pocket. "Come."

She walked fast, an urgency in her stride that surprised me.

"You know about our, uh, mission?" Weir asked, keeping easy pace with her.

"I know enough. Not many do, even in the guard. But I'm also an advisor to Queen Asteria on certain matters. And the matter of the lost coven, the rogue fae, the nexus of magic...well, the courts refuse to intervene, of course."

Of course. The faerie courts were very clear about not interfering—or even pretending to care—about the matters of the earthbound fae. As far as they were concerned, they'd written us off when they'd left the human realm and created the veils that separated the worlds. We were, as the courts saw these matters, on our own.

Which made this encounter far too strange. And only underscored the importance of rescuing the coven and defeating Weylin once and for all.

"There's a 'but' coming, isn't there?" Weir asked.

Our elven captor-turned-possible-rescuer shot him a look like he'd sprouted a second head, no doubt finding his human turn of phrase odd. But she answered as we ascended a curved stone staircase. "But...I suspect the courts could view holding you captive in the Summer Queen's dungeon as interfering. That is up to the queen herself to decide for certain, though."

With that, she fell silent—the kind of silence that suggested she'd say no more on the subject.

We walked down a long hallway, the walls covered in a living tapestry of ivy, and she opened a door to a simple but tidy room—likely a servant's quarters. "I'll have to lock the door behind you, of course, but I'll have someone bring you fresh garments and something to eat and drink."

"And if anyone stops by to ask what we're doing locked in the castle?" I dared to say. "What should we tell them?"

Her green eyes locked with mine. My raven flapped her wings, wanting to fly from the intensity of that gaze. "Tell them that you are *guests* of Brenna of the queen's guard."

With that, she ushered us inside. The door shut softly, the distinct sound of a lock clicking into place sounding behind her.

***

Weir

Nothing about this was good. I mean, it was better than being in the dungeon, but we were still being held captive.

And Siobhan—who claimed she'd been sent by the Willow Creek Coven to rescue me—had hidden her true identity.

Funny thing was, I always trusted my instincts about people—magical or otherwise. And Siobhan?

I could feel the walls she'd built up around herself, miles upon miles of them. But she didn't feel dangerous. I sensed no malice, no meanness in her.

There was a vulnerability in her, tucked safely behind those walls.

I spun away from the door, its oaken surface polished to a shine. Siobhan stared out the window, curtains of gauzy pale green billowing in a warm breeze. Her forehead was furrowed in a scowl, her arms crossed over her chest.

"This wasn't part of your plan, was it?" I asked, joining her at the window.

She turned that scowl on me. "No."

I nodded. "Were you telling the truth? About how quickly we need to return to Willow Creek?"

"Yes." The word was a mere whisper, dripping with sadness.

I wanted to demand the truth, but now wasn't the time. I didn't know why she'd pretend to be a witch when she was full-fae, but I supposed she had her reasons.

And if those reasons were sinister?

Well, she could've killed me in my sleep last night—I'd likely have slept through anything, I'd slept so soundly on the forest floor. She probably could've vanished this morning and left me to my fate with the queen's guard, but she hadn't. So, whatever her true purpose was, I had to believe that Siobhan was on the coven's side.

She sniffed, turning away from me with her back stiff.

I placed my hand on her shoulder. "What's wrong?"

She shook her head, but didn't turn to face me. "I've failed at everything I've tried to accomplish since I set foot in Willow Creek."

"Ah. Well, if it makes you feel any better, nothing I've done recently has been a rip-roaring success. I got lost in the Mountain Pass when I was supposed to be looking for a doorway back to Willow Creek."

She spun around to face me, her eyes glinting. "That's different. I'm supposed to be—" She waved her arm around, gesturing toward the sky. "—fated, or whatever."

"What exactly is this fate you keep talking about?"

She shook her head. "Forget it."

"Siobhan," I said, stepping forward. I didn't want to push, but neither of us knew what would happen next, me least of all. I had questions that needed to be answered. "My mother and my sister are still out there somewhere. My entire coven could be destroyed. And now you tell me Weylin could destroy not just the coven, but the entire town of Willow Creek. So, no, I can't forget it. And I can't exactly be a good ally to you if I don't know the whole truth."

She glared at me, an eyebrow arched sharply, but it was the sort of look that I had quickly come to realize meant she thought I was making a good point.

"Why don't we sit?" I said, gesturing to the foot of the bed. It was a surprisingly intimate arrangement, but it would have to do.

She shrugged, but I could see the exhaustion weighing her down as we sat at the foot of the bed, across from a simple painting of a sprawling oak tree, the colors splashed across the canvas impossibly vivid.

"Everything here is so bright," I observed.

"That's the Summer Realm for you," she said. "Shiny and gleaming on the surface..."

"But underneath?"

"Everyone has their own designs. That's important to remember about the fae. The fae have their own motivations, and what humans want rarely matters to them."

Ah. I was getting somewhere. Slowly, we were circling the truth. I took a risk and took her hand, sliding my thumb over hers.

"And you? What do you want?" I said, keeping my voice low.

She sighed. I felt the rush of tension leaving her body. "It's more of what I don't want." Her gaze locked with mine—intense, fierce. "I don't want to be the one in the prophecy. I don't want this mantle they've draped over my shoulders since I was still in my mother's womb."

Whatever I'd been expecting her to confess, that certainly wasn't it. "That would be rough."

"Yeah," she said, rolling her eyes. "I know exactly how it goes—word for word."

"*And where the willow weeps against flowing waters, currents of magic run deep,*" she intoned. "*The son's betrayal lies beneath the sacred earth. And the fae daughter, raven born of wolf, descended from the sacred rose, shall seek the key. And the tower, where the lost witches wait, will yield, and she will guide them through the door. And upon the black moon, shall the magic meet its mark.*"

She squeezed her eyes shut, deep furrows etched into her brow.

I couldn't help it. The first time I saw her, she'd looked so fierce. And now? In this moment, she looked so vulnerable. I drew her into my arms.

"That's a lot to carry," I said.

"I keep messing up," she whispered as she snuggled deeper in my embrace, accepting the sanctuary I offered.

"What do you mean?" I asked, adjusting slightly so her head could rest more easily on my chest.

"Every spell I cast, every decision I make seems to take me further from rescuing the coven and defeating Weylin, not closer."

"I mean, it's a prophecy, right?" I reasoned. "So, maybe everything that seems like a misstep is really part of some greater plan. Me stepping through your doorway and bringing us here. Being brought here to the Summer Queen's castle. Even something as simple as us meeting could be..." I swallowed hard. No. I might've been the son of a seer and the brother of an empath, but I couldn't bring myself to suggest that fate meant for me and Siobhan to be anything other than accidental companions on a magical detour.

She sniffed and drew away from my embrace, crossing her arms over her chest. "Like you're my pre-destined magical sidekick?"

"Hey," I said. "I am not your sidekick. But I do wish you'd stop pretending to be a witch."

Her eyes widened, the color draining from her face. She stood, her back now broomstick straight, and approached the painting across the room, studying it with intent. After a moment, she turned back to me and shrugged. "So I'm not a witch. I'm a faerie, through and through."

"Why did you lie?" I asked.

"You don't understand," she said, clenching her fists at her sides. "Every moment of my life has been planned out for me. Every lesson. Every day. Every trip. Every encounter. And so, when it came time for me to come to Willow Creek? Nothing I've done since I arrived was my decision."

"Shit," I said.

"Yeah." She nodded, the single word a breathless exhale. Then she gave me a wicked grin. "If our magical mishap did anything, though, it gave me one thing. This—" she gestured to the room around us—"wasn't part of the plan. So, for a few moments, at least, I get to decide my own fate."

She crossed the room and took my hands, her eyes wild. "Thank you for that, at least, Weir."

My heart thundered, its beat as wild as the look in her eyes. Her whole life had been carefully choreographed. What would that be like? Never being able to make a single decision for yourself? She must've felt so trapped.

Heat sizzled inside of me. I wanted to kiss her. I could see it in her eyes, the slow, deliberate way she licked her lips, parting them slightly. She wanted it too.

I slid one hand up to cup her the back of her neck, using the other to tilt her chin up to meet my lips.

I met hers softly at first, but with a moan she crushed her lips to mine, deepening it.

A knock sounded at the door.

We flew apart, like two birds startled out of a tree. The door opened to reveal Brenna and a young woman dressed in loose-fitting brown pants and an ivory shirt tucked in. She carried a tray of food. A young man in similar garb carried a stack of clothes.

"The queen is in a meeting," Brenna said. "But she's aware of your arrival and has promised to see you soon—within the hour, I should expect." Her sharp gaze traveled from me to Siobhan, a quick quirk of her lips telling me she knew she'd walked in on something intimate.

The servants deposited their burdens and retreated. With a curt nod to both of us, Brenna departed as well. The lock clicked into place behind the trio.

I glanced at Siobhan, but she was already pouring a cup of tea from the green teapot. "Mmm. Bitterwort. Don't let the name fool you." She filled the second cup to the brim and handed it to me. "You'll love it. It has a rich, earthy flavor."

"Siobhan..." I said, feeling like I should say something about what just happened—however tragically brief the encounter might've been.

She shook her head, smiling at me over the brim of her cup. "I'm liking this whole deciding my own fate thing."

I couldn't forget my family, my coven, or my drive to get back home. But I returned her mischievous smile, and then took a sip of the tea. It was good, like she said—earthy, grounding.

I knew Siobhan wouldn't let herself be distracted for too long from her mission. It simply wasn't in her nature—prophecy or not.

But if she needed this brief respite from whatever lay ahead on our journey, then so be it.

Chapter Ten

Siobhan

The memory of that kiss lingered on my lips. Weir was so unlike anyone I'd ever met. Wildly attractive I was used to—the fae weren't always enchantingly beautiful, of course, but many were. And magic? Oh, that I was used to as well.

But he had this way of slipping past my defenses. That should've scared me—I'd been trained all my life to not let anyone too close. Closeness could lead to betrayal, I'd always been reminded. And my mission was far too important to take that risk.

No one had more on the line than Weir in this situation, though. His family was trapped, his coven at risk.

I had to trust him. More than had to. I *did* trust him. He prodded me with questions about the fae and the prophecy as we ate, our meal a simple stew of summer vegetable and venison, served with a hearty soda bread. Talking with him felt natural, and I could almost forget how terribly off course I'd let everything get.

Or the fact that back in Willow Creek, I would face some very angry witches whom I'd lied to and stolen from.

One secret I didn't share, though. Not the prophecy itself, but what the fae had planned for after it was fulfilled. Because even Weir, kind though he was, wouldn't go along with what the earthbound fae had planned for the Crossroads of Magic. After fighting for their very existence from one faerie, there was no way they'd give up that power, that magic so easily to another, not even if the earthbound fae had every intention of merely preserving its magic.

But the Rose had made it clear. What happened in Willow Creek never would've occurred if fae sisters Kalann and Ananene hadn't abandoned their posts. The Rose wanted the Crossroads of Magic under fae protection again—end of discussion.

No. That was a secret I couldn't divulge—not yet. Maybe not ever. I'd let the Rose or one of the other fae deliver that news themselves.

For now, I was in the Summer Realm, sharing a meal with a handsome man whose kiss had made my head spin. I was going to enjoy the moment while it lasted, like plucking a fresh raspberry from among the thorns, savoring its sweetness.

Except...I couldn't enjoy the moment. Not fully.

I thrust my teacup aside and rose, fighting the urge to pace the room nervously. I was earthbound fae, trespassing in the Summer Realm and demanding an audience with the queen herself. Just because that audience was being granted didn't mean things would go my way.

"We should probably get dressed," I said. "Brenna will be back soon."

Weir nodded, his brow furrowing. "Exactly how worried should I be?"

I unfurled the garments the servants had brought us, pondering how to answer that question. "I don't know. The whole situation. It's complicated."

"I think we're at another point where I could use an explanation."

He wasn't wrong. With a sigh, I thrust a set of garments at him. "Here, change into this. I'll explain, I swear."

Weir disappeared behind the privacy screen, a simple wooden trifold screen with vines carved in the top. Even the simplest rooms of the Summer Queen's castle had an earthy elegance to them, polished wood and vibrant greens making everything feel bright.

With Weir ensconced behind the screen, I tugged my peasant top over my head and shimmied out of my jeans. "Fae and humans used to live together. But as the human population grew, most of the fae used an ancient, powerful magic to create their own realms. Some of the fae—a very small number of us—stayed behind, choosing to live among humans. They call us the earthbound fae. Many of the fae who aren't earthbound...they don't trust us. The Summer Queen is one of those. So we technically need permission to enter this realm or to live here permanently."

"Permission that you don't have?"

"Exactly." I stepped into the garments that had been provided to me—a calf-length dress in delicate shade of periwinkle made of gauzy fabric similar to linen but with a silvery sheen. Not something I would've chosen myself, but a suitable outfit for begging the Summer Queen's forgiveness.

I removed my labradorite pendant and added the key to chain, then refastened it around my neck. The chain was long enough that I could tuck both the pendant and—more importantly—the key under the neckline of the dress, the billowy fabric ensuring they stayed hidden.

"So, what uh..." He paused, flinging the shirt I'd conjured for him over the privacy screen. His arm stretched up as he slid into the new, much more formal attire. "What exactly is the punishment for trespassing?"

I surveyed myself in the mirror, frowning. "I don't know. Queen Asteria, she, well...it's always different. I mean, from what I hear, she's fair. But you have to remember, what seems like a fair punishment to a faerie queen can seem outrageous to those of us who are used to the human world."

Weir emerged from behind the screen.

"Wow," I said, then felt myself turning a violent shade of crimson.

Weir grinned and adjusted his shirt sleeves. The shirt was midnight black with leather ties at its V-neck, and he'd replaced his pants with the kilt they'd brought him—only instead of a Scottish tartan, it was a mossy green embroidered with black vines.

"Wow yourself, by the way," he said, his grin deepening as he studied me.

When our eyes locked, though, it wasn't mirth I saw there. There was desire, molten, scarcely contained. But something darker too.

I stepped toward him, my breath catching. "What?"

"I had a vision. Well, one my mother, a seer, shared with me. And I saw you. Or someone who looked an awful lot like you. We were in a temple in a forest, and the woman was wearing that dress." He swallowed.

I didn't break eye contact, just moved toward him. "I guess that's a good sign, right? That we'll get out of this, that we won't be stuck in a dungeon somewhere?"

He nodded. The heat of his gaze sizzled right to my core, warmth sliding up my thighs to pool at the apex of my legs, my lips tingling as if he'd kissed me again. Being trapped in a room with this man wasn't exactly doing wonders for my self-control.

I turned away. "They'll be back soon," I said, fussing with the folds of the dress. I wasn't used to something so formal, so feminine, though I had to admit I was enjoying Weir's reaction.

Maybe a little too much, given our present circumstances.

Weir nodded. "Right. Should we...do we need a plan? You're the expert here, after all."

I couldn't help laughing. "The thing to remember about Queen Asteria is that she's as unpredictable as a summer thunderstorm. There's no way we can plan for whatever she's going to throw at us because there's no way to predict what she'll do. I doubt even her closest advisors could do that, let alone a little earthbound raven like myself."

His brow furrowed again, knitting into that mixture of concern and concentration. "Okay. So, we just..."

I smiled. I could feel his nerves jangling, but if we stayed here in silence, pent-up desire would replace those nerves. And as tempting as that sounded, it was a terrible idea. "I've told you about myself. Tell me about you."

The furrows in his brow vanished. He quirked a dark eyebrow. "Me? What's there to tell? My family moved to Willow Creek a couple years ago. My parents owned a two-hundred acre horse farm in another part of the state, but they wanted a change. My sister...she was struggling. She's an empath, and got bullied a lot in high school. College overwhelmed her. My parents wanted to slow down, but my mom also wanted my sister to be around other witches. She thought it would be easier for Winnie if there was a magical community who could truly understand her gift.

"At least, that's the reason my parents gave for us moving to Willow Creek. In reality, my mom's a seer, so she might have had other reasons."

He settled onto the edge of the bed, tracing the embroidery in the green coverlet. I came to sit beside him.

"Do they still have horses then—your parents, I mean?" I prompted.

"We have six horses, yeah. Mom runs a farrier business, so that keeps her pretty busy. Winnie spends a lot of time around animals—not just the horses, but cats, dogs, rabbits. She says their emotions are easier to process than humans, so it's not as intense."

"You're very protective of her," I guessed.

"Yeah. She's getting stronger, but her abilities can overwhelm her at times."

"What about you?" I couldn't help but asking. "Tell me about your magic. I know you can shift."

He stared straight ahead, as if seeing something I couldn't. "That's the thing. I don't know. I am a witch. I have earth magic. I've done some basic spells. But maybe...maybe the truth of my magic is deeper than even I know."

"Hmm..." I wondered how to respond to that. The witches of Willow Creek definitely had their share of mysteries, didn't they?

But Weir? He was the mystery I was most interested in solving.

A knock sounded at the door. We both jumped up. I nervously smoothed my dress as Weir went to answer it.

Brenna entered, not even bothering with a greeting.

"Queen Asteria will see you now."

***

Weir

We followed Brenna down a long hallway, up one set of stairs and down another. The passages of the castle had wide windows overlooking sprawling gardens. The skies were blue and cloudless today, sunlight glinting off the shimmering stone buildings and highlighting the sparkling fountains.

But I couldn't shake the sense of dread that coiled in my gut.

Siobhan held her head high as we followed Brenna through the twisting halls of the castle, but the hard set of her jaw told me she was just as nervous as I was.

We stopped in front of a tall set of polished wooden doors—at least two stories high, with intricate carvings of vines.

Brenna stopped and eyed us both. "Once you pass beyond these doors, there's nothing more I can do for you," she said, her tone matter of fact.

I gulped. "Any advice?" I asked as a bead of sweat trickled down the back of my neck. I offered her a sheepish grin she didn't return.

"Choose your words carefully." There was no humor in her voice. She leaned in, glancing around us and keeping her voice low. "If you are who you say you are, if your mission is as you say, tread carefully. Weylin Felson has allies amongst the summer fae."

With a bow, she strode down the hall and disappeared around a corner. Before I could say anything, the doors swung open, seemingly of their own volition.

This was it. Here I was, a mere mortal lost in the faerie realms, about to meet the Summer Queen.

And somehow, this moment seemed worse than the trolls in the Winter Realm, worse than those endless days and nights spent wandering cluelessly in the Mountain Pass.

Siobhan took a few steps into the chamber, and I followed. She no doubt knew the protocols here better than I did, so I'd just follow her lead. Probably my best chance of escaping an eternity locked in the queen's dungeon.

The room had a round glass ceiling that offered a view of the sky, the floor smooth marble shimmering with hints of green, blue, and gold. A living tapestry of vines climbed up the walls.

And at the far end of the room rested a throne of branches, vines, and roses, in the center of which sat a woman whose aura left no doubt as to her identity: the Summer Queen.

The air buzzed with electricity and ancient magic as we approached. It danced along my skin, as if lightning had struck nearby. With her blond hair in its tight braid and her violet eyes, her cheekbones sharp angles, her lips the color of a freshly bloomed rose, she looked every bit *La Belle Dame sans Merci*. Her emerald green dress glittered as though speckled with stardust—and for all I knew, maybe it was.

The expression on her face didn't exactly scream warmth and understanding for our plight.

Siobhan crossed the wide expanse of the room swiftly and fell to one knee. "Queen Asteria, brightest blessings from the earthbound fae," she said, her voice a touch breathless, as though she recited a long-ago memorized script.

I followed, bowing. "Queen Asteria, I..." I fumbled for the next words.

"Queen of Leaf and Bloom, Queen of Sunshine and Thunder, it is my pleasure to introduce my companion," Siobhan quickly finished for me. "Meet Weir Delaney of the Witches of Willow Creek. He joins me on a mission—"

"Enough." Queen Asteria waved a hand, and Siobhan quieted. She peered down at us from the throne. "If you are earthbound fae, you should know that the summer fae do not permit your presence in our realm except for those occasions when *we* deem it necessary or warranted—or on those days when the veil between our worlds thins enough that we cannot prevent your entry. Today is not such a day—and I don't recall any of my advisors alerting me to any necessary circumstances."

Her words had an edge, like shards of glass. As she spoke, the skies darkened, a jagged bolt of lightning darting through the sky above.

Siobhan rose, bowing her head. "Queen Asteria, we beg your pardon. When I parted the veil, I meant to enter the Winter Realm, where the laws permit the earthbound fae to come and go."

"Oh?" The queen's nostrils flared. "And are you so unskilled in rudimentary magic that you entered my realm by mistake?"

"No. My lady..." Siobhan faltered.

"That was my fault," I interjected.

Both sets of eyes turned to me. The queen looked intrigued, cocking her head. Siobhan, on the other hand, turned pale, her eyes widening.

"You interfered in faerie magic?" she asked. "Such a mortal thing as yourself, your magic so small? Tell me how."

Choose your words carefully. Brenna's warning thundered in my head. Well, I wasn't going to lie to the faerie queen.

"I don't know how exactly. I was lost in the Winter Realm, longing for a glimpse of sunshine. I saw a portal open, and I leapt through it. It brought me here—and Siobhan, to both our surprise."

The queen leaned forward, bringing her forearms to rest on her thighs. "And you don't know how you did such a thing?"

I shook my head. "I don't."

"Hmm." Her gaze darted between me and Siobhan. Judging from that look, wheels were turning in her head. I wasn't sure that would be to our benefit.

"Queen Asteria, Lady of the Vine and the Thorn, please," Siobhan said. "We are on a mission. The witches of Willow Creek are—"

"I know of the witches of Willow Creek," the queen snapped. "I know of the Crossroads, and of the Guardian's plight. I don't need you, of all beings, to fill me in on such things."

She rose from her throne and approached us. Thunder rumbled so intensely it shook the castle, lightning flashing overhead. Hail bounced off the glass ceiling above, a storm no doubt made of the Summer Queen's wrath.

Too stunned to speak, I trembled, my skin feeling suddenly hot and my stomach now churning. Was it her wrath that worried me, or the amount of faerie magic swirling in the air that made me feel so ill?

She studied me. "If you did this, Weir of the Willow Creek Witches, then by your hand must it be undone." She turned to Siobhan. "And as for you, your powers will be bound while in my realm. Neither of you will return without my blessing. You have until nightfall to open a doorway and leave the Summer Realm. If not, the dungeons will have to suffice."

Siobhan took a step backward. "My lady, for a witch, opening such a doorway for the first time can be a difficult task. And certain magical tools are required."

"That, little raven, is not my problem." The queen pressed her thumb and middle finger together and gave them a snap.

It looked like our conversation was over.

Part Three: Earthbound Magic

"Beyond the gate
Beyond the root
The tree shall sing
Now look within."
—Tangled Souls

Chapter Eleven

Weir

The floor fell away. Colors swirled around me, inky shadows mixed with flecks of green and streaks of sky blue and sunny gold.

I hit hard earth with a thud that took my breath away. When I blinked, a stormy sky loomed above, wide and gnarled trees surrounding us.

I sat up, rubbing my head, only to see Siobhan in a crouch position.

"How do you do that?" I said. "Always land on your feet?"

She shrugged. "Years of training."

I snorted. I knew she wasn't joking. "So your training wasn't just magical in nature, then? You had, what, combat training too?"

"Yes. In addition to studying human witchcraft and faerie magic—and the corresponding lore—my daily lessons involved basic self-defense skills."

"Noted." Was there anything she couldn't do?

She rose gracefully, the dress with its shimmering fabric rippling in the breeze. My breath caught, gut clenching as I stared up at her. She was the whole package, wasn't she? Strong. Fierce. Funny. Witty. Brave.

I rose, brushing myself off. "Are we still in the Summer Realm? This place looks—and feels—different." Kind of spooky, if I was being completely honest.

"Yeah." She glanced around, her gaze lingering on the dark clouds above. "The Summer Realm is vast, and some corners in particular are much wilder. The magic here has an edge to it. Even summer has its shadows, you know?"

"I can see that," I said.

The air was warm, a bit sticky against my skin, but the breeze held the promise of storms to come. One nearby tree was charred, as if struck by lightning at some point. Everything was green, but even the vines had obvious thorns. Nothing here was soft, welcoming, or serene.

Siobhan worried her labradorite pendant between her fingers.

"Did she really do it?" I said. "Take your magic, I mean."

She nodded. "It's not gone, technically. It's like she put a sleeping-beauty curse on my faerie magic, including my raven." She stepped forward, her hand coming to rest on my cheek. "It is possible to open the doorway with witchcraft, you know."

"I'm not..." I turned away, raking my hands through my hair. How could I explain to her that I, a member of the Willow Creek Coven, didn't really practice witchcraft? "Look, I've got no problem with witchcraft. I just...I always leaned into my shifter side. It sounds ridiculous now, but growing up, my shifter magic was the one thing that was mine. Winnie was an empath who struggled with being in the same room with anyone. Mom was a seer that people came to for guidance. I just figured witchcraft was their thing and shifter magic was mine."

"So you never learned?" she asked. There was no judgment in her tone. Only concern.

And I got it. At nightfall, we'd both turn into pumpkins and be tossed, unceremoniously, into Queen Asteria's dungeon.

If that happened, by the time we got home, centuries would've passed. If we *ever* got to return home. Willow Creek, my family, everyone and everything I loved would've been long gone.

"I know the basics, but beyond that, not much," I admitted.

To her credit, Siobhan merely shrugged. "Okay. Time to learn. I might not be a witch, and my magic might work differently, but maybe Aunt Fiona's lessons will come in handy for more than just pretending to be a witch after all."

I smiled.

"What?" she said, quirking that left eyebrow sharply.

"I like that, you know. How you just spring into action. And don't say it's your training, either. It's you. You're clever. You're strong. You roll with the punches. It's not your destiny, Siobhan. It's just who you are."

She turned away, smoothing the already smooth material of her dress. "Well, then," she said, clearing her throat. "Let's get started."

"You're the teacher, then," I said. I couldn't help but grin, adding, "And I'm the student."

Her lips fluttered into a smile, but she shook her head. "I suspect we'll quickly grow tired of each other's company if we're locked in a dungeon, so if we want to find out where that kiss earlier leads, we'd better focus."

"Right," I said. Like I needed a reminder of the fate that would befall us. "No pressure, then."

She sighed. "I'm sorry. I'm not...I guess I'd hoped my magical lesson days were behind me." She exhaled, tucking her short, choppy blond hair behind her ear. "Let's start over. Let's kneel and place our hand against the earth."

Siobhan knelt, the slits in the dress allowing her to bend. I knew she'd probably rather be wearing anything but that formal dress, but the color really did suit her. And the material, the way it highlighted her curves...

I swallowed and knelt as well, pressing a palm to the green but rough grass beneath our feet.

"Breathe in," she said, her eyes drifting closed. "Let the energy of the earth flow into your body. Feel her magic, ancient and wild. Feel the tendrils of magic moving up your arm, all through your body."

I did as she instructed. It was a simple enough magical exercise, one that was suppose to ground the magical practitioner while opening them up as a conduit to magic. Releasing the tether of the mundane world while increasing the connection to the mystical one.

It took a few breaths in and out to clear my head. Siobhan kept talking, her tone low, her accent lilting, drawing me into a trance. At first, I felt nothing. I knew how to ground, but I'd never really felt the "tingles of energy" that other witches talked about when they practiced magic.

I pressed my palm harder into the earth.

Focus. You can do this. Magic 101.

Nothing. No tingles, no tiny jolts of electricity. No tendrils of magic. No mystical current or connection.

"It's not working," I said, drawing my hand away with a groan. "However I connect to my magic, this isn't it."

Siobhan frowned, but rose, offering me her hand. "Tell me, when you do spells or a ritual, how do you feel?"

"Well, like a follower, honestly. I never lead a ritual. I've only done spells with only witches present. And it feels...kind of warm at times, but not...I just don't think I experience magic the same way other witches do. I guess it's because I'm only half-witch. The other half of my magic is shifter magic."

"Hmm." She crossed her arms over her chest, pacing. "I haven't studied shifter magic very much. My raven shifter ability is fae magic, not human."

"Do you suppose there's much difference?" I asked. I couldn't help but be intrigued. "Between a fae shifter and a human shifter?"

"There are some. I don't have to disrobe before I shift, unlike a human shifter. We suspect it's because of the fae ability to conjure and create glamours. Almost an extension of that magic."

"I wish that were the case for me. Especially when I first started shifting, I ended up in some pretty awkward situations."

She chuckled. "I can imagine."

We both grew quiet. She paced, obviously deep in thought. I held my palms outward, searching for any sign that I could sense the magic in the air. It should be possible. No, more than possible. It should be simple—second-nature, even.

"Why can't I do this?" I said.

"I have a theory," Siobhan said. "What if your shifter magic is dominant, and it's sort of blocking your witchcraft?"

"It makes sense, but how would we solve a problem like that. I mean, that sounds like a pretty serious roadblock given our current circumstances."

"You're assuming that one has to lead." She held out both hands, bringing her left in front of her right. "Imagine your shifter magic is my left hand. Your witchcraft is my right. We don't need to bring your witchcraft here—" she brought her right hand in front. "We need to bring them both here." She brought both hands side by side. "Working in harmony. Shifter magic cooperating with witchcraft."

"That makes sense, I guess." I hesitated. Because it didn't really seem like a problem we had a solution for—or, at least, one we could implement in the middle of a spooky faerie forest.

Siobhan fell quiet. I tried to let her think. I walked toward one of the trees—a gnarled tree as wide a car, its leaves bright green.

Between Siobhan's theory and my mom's words during our brief time together in the Crossroads of Magic, there had to be a solution. There was a missing link, I was sure of it.

"You know, my aunt is a shifter," I said. "A horse shifter. We thought maybe, since I had shifter magic, that would be my animal form too. I grew up on a farm, I've been around horses all my life. It makes sense, you know?"

"But you're not a horse shifter. You're a puma."

I nodded. "Exactly. And your shifter form is a raven. And even with your fae magic, that's the only animal form you can take?"

"Yes..." She squinted at me, but didn't argue, just crossed her arms over her chest again and waited.

"After I shifted for the first time, we did some research. It turns out, our animal form isn't a coincidence, and it's not genetic. The animal form we take is connected to something, some aspect of ourselves. You're a raven. And it suits you. Clever. Resourceful. Adaptable. And maybe a bit of a trickster when the situation calls for it."

Her squint turned into a glare. "I'm not sure I like where this is heading."

"Hey, I like that about you. It might just save all our asses," I said, giving her my sexiest grin.

She rolled her eyes, but gave me a little flick of her wrist. "Fine. No offense taken."

"So, if my shifter magic and my witchy side are connected..." I trailed off.

"Then maybe, since you're half-witch and half-shifter, your magical ability is linked to your puma magic," Siobhan finished, a glimmer of understanding in her eyes.

"If we figure out why my inner shifter choose the puma form, we might find the key to unlocking my inner witch's earth magic."

***

Siobhan

I frowned.

"You're wrong," I said, in that blunt, cutting tone that drove my cousins crazy.

For perhaps the first time since we'd met, irritation filled Weir's face, though it was quickly replaced by a stubborn scowl. "I think we should at least try it."

"No, I don't mean..." I gave a heavy sigh of frustration. Forcing myself to use a softer tone, I continued. "I think your theory is good. But I mean, you're wrong about why I shift into a raven. It's not about the traits most people associate with ravens. Or their personalities. Well, maybe it is, a little. But there's something deeper."

I paused, gathering myself. I studied the gathering storm clouds above. Of course, Queen Asteria couldn't just send us to the creepiest, most shadowy part of the Summer Realm. She had to send rain.

Could've been worse, though. There were worse things than a torrential downpour.

Weir stood in stoic silence, watching me. No one back home ever waited out one of my silences. It was always, *Oh, she's in one of her moods—again.* Or a quick and easy reason why I was wrong, how much I had to learn.

But with Weir, he waited for me to prepare myself, to gather myself enough to share my secret.

That's how I knew he was the one I wanted to share it with.

I approached him, took his hand, and forced myself to look him in the eye. "When I'm a raven, no one tells me what to do. When I'm a raven, I can fly, cry out, perch in the branches, soar over the earth. When I'm a raven, I have a freedom I don't have in my normal life. That's what I remember about the first time I shifted. We all knew I had the ability. My cousins had been teasing me—they're older, always thinking they know everything. My aunt wouldn't listen to me. My lessons had gone terribly that day. I stormed out, and the shift just swept over me. I was gone for hours—my family was furious. But I felt so free. That's why I'm a raven. Because they symbolize magic *and* freedom."

His gaze was soft as he stared down at me. The back of his hand brushed my cheek. "I get it. And you deserve that freedom. To make your own choices. They never should've tried to control you like that."

"They wanted what was best for me," I said. But honestly? I wasn't so sure. I knew my family loved me, but sometimes, it felt like the prophecy came first. I was the fated one first, and Siobhan O'Shea second. "I complain, but I know they love me. It just...we're fae. Prophecies are important."

"So are choices," he said, tilting my chin toward his face.

He kissed me deeply. We barely tore ourselves away. It would be too easy to lose ourselves in the desire building between us.

But I did have to fulfill the prophecy. There was literally no one else, at this moment, who could. And Weir? Well, there was no one but him who could open that doorway and get us out of here.

"We'll have time for that soon enough," I said, drawing myself away reluctantly.

He sighed, the sound slow and languid. He nodded. "Agreed." His tone was rough with pent-up desire.

I felt the same, the heat and pressure building between my legs. But we couldn't. Not here. Not now.

"It's your turn, Weir," I said. "Tell me about the first time you shifted. When you became a puma. What did it feel like. We have to figure out why your inner shifter chose that form for you."

He took my hand and guided me to a nearby boulder to sit. We settled, and he clasped his hands on his knees, staring down into them as if they held a deep well of memories.

"I was fifteen. Winnie was fourteen. She was a really sweet, shy kid, and kids in school bullied her relentlessly. What made it worse was that she's an empath, so she felt not just how they felt about her, but how they felt about themselves."

"Mom pulled her out of school to homeschool her. It was a hard time for me. I ran cross-country, so I still went to school. Everyone asked about Winnie, and I couldn't say much.

"One day, I was walking on this hiking trail not far from our house—way out in the mountains, really off-the-beaten path. And I felt...lost. Scared for my sister. I wanted to help her, to make her life easier.

He sniffed, but continued. "And then the change came over me. There was this series of shivers, and I looked down, and I saw these sandy paws on the autumn earth. The scent of fallen leaves, of recent rain, everything was sharper. There was this clarity."

He closed his eyes, inhaling, as if relieving the moment. His story was so raw, so vivid, that I felt like I was there on that autumn path with him, a newly shifted puma in the wild forest for the first time.

"And?" I whispered, though I scarcely dared.

"And then I saw these...silvery edges. The world blurred a bit. I ran. The scent changed, became wilder somehow. I was in a meadow of flowers, a place I'd never been even though I hiked that trail dozens of times. I knew somehow I'd never find that place again. There were flowers in all these hues—golden yellows, purples, crimson red, burnt orange. Somehow—I don't know how—I managed to pluck one with my teeth. The petals were this deep purple, almost like an iris, but the flower looked more like some sort of lily. Then, the world shimmered again. I made my way home through the forests. Mom looked out the kitchen window—she was doing the dishes. She screamed.

"She and Dad and Winnie came running out. I couldn't figure out how to shift back. I was scared. What if they thought I was a threat?"

"Did they?" I asked, though based on what he'd told me about his family, I already knew the answer.

"Dad took one look at me and laughed. He said, 'Sarah, I do believe that puma's got a flower in its mouth.' And they all stared at me, and Winnie screamed, 'It's Weir.'"

I couldn't help smiling. "Your family sounds wonderful."

His eyes filled with tears, but they didn't fall. He squeezed my hand. "They are. And they'll love you. And I think you'll love them."

"I'll meet them soon," I said. I didn't dare to think otherwise.

It wasn't just my fate now, not just some mission I was assigned.

Now that I'd met Weir, it was a choice. I would rescue the Willow Creek Coven not just because it was prophesized but because I had to do it—for him. And for myself. I turned his story over and over in my head.

I'd been focused on the part about his family, but that wasn't the important part—not this precise moment, anyway.

"Weir, do you know what your story means? What your gift is now?"

He cocked his head. "Did I...walk between the worlds?"

I laughed. "Yeah. I'm pretty sure you did."

Chapter Twelve

Weir

A single, fat drop of rain fell from the sky, slapping against my hand.

In hindsight, my latest revelation seemed obvious. But at the time, I'd been more focused on learning how to shift and shift back again. The idea that I'd crossed into a faerie realm never even occurred to me.

I remembered that purple flower that I'd clutched in my teeth. Winnie had kept it in a vase on her windowsill, her pain eased slightly by what she called 'the most beautiful flower ever.' Its colors stayed vivid long after it should've wilted and browned.

Faerie magic, I supposed.

"So, what now?" I asked, breaking the spell of silence that had fallen over us. Another raindrop plopped against my head, trailing down my cheek.

"Well, it sounds like you can access the magic most easily when in your puma form. I'd suggest you shift. You're not going to use magic to open a doorway. Instead, you'll walk, searching for a place where the veil is thin. I've crossed between the realms this way on Samhain—Halloween. On certain days, the veil is thin in more places. But sometimes, like now, there are only a few spots. In your puma form, maybe you can find those places and cross through."

Her explanation made sense, little as I knew about crossing between the human world and the faerie realms.

"Do you think that's why I was able to hijack your door? Because I was in my shifter form when I saw it?"

Siobhan rubbed her amulet, the bluish-green stone shimmering like water in the sparsely falling rain. "I think that might be part of it. Maybe. I think...I think we were both wishing for something at that moment, and our magic collided and got all tangled up."

I nodded. "The faerie raven and the witch puma."

I rose, offering her a hand. "You do look beautiful, you know. Like you're on your way to a faerie ball."

"And you look dashing in your kilt," she said, smiling. For once, she didn't turn her face away or blush when I complimented her. Something had shifted between us in this moment, changed in a way from which we could never return.

Siobhan stood there as a few drops of rain fell around her, a vision in her shimmering dress.

The vision...

"I think I know where we need to go," I said. "In the vision my mother shared with me, there was a temple. Kind of crumbling, this ancient stone place. If we find it, maybe that's where the veil is thinnest. Maybe that's why I saw it."

Thunder rumbled overhead. Siobhan closed her eyes. "I don't think that's a coincidence. We'd better hurry. And not just because of the storm."

"Why, then?" I pressed. "We have until sunset. That's a few hours, at least."

"Weir..." her tone was low, warning, all the earlier playfulness vanished. Her piercing eyes were as dark as the storm clouds above. "I think we need to get out of the Summer Realm as soon as possible. I didn't want to say anything until we'd figured out how to unlock your magic, but something isn't right. I mean, I know my magic is asleep, but my intuition is telling me not to trust this place."

"Okay." I nodded. I trusted Siobhan's intuition—probably more than I trusted my own. "I'll shift. Follow me and stay close, okay? If I find a place to crossover, just follow me. Promise?"

"Oh, I promise. I don't plan on coming back to the Summer Realm for a long, long time."

I wanted to ask her what she planned. After all this was over, would she stay in Willow Creek? Would she return to her family's village in Ireland, her mission complete? Or would she vanish from my life, striking out on her own to embrace her newfound independence?

I couldn't bring myself to ask, though. Probably because I didn't want to know the answer. But also because it didn't matter. Not yet. Not until we escaped the Summer Realm and reunited the coven. Not until we defeated Weylin and saved Willow Creek and the Crossroads of Magic.

And our success in any of those endeavors was far, far from certain.

But first things first.

I stripped out of my clothes and folded them. Siobhan turned away.

"I'll carry those for you, just in case you need them again," she called over her shoulder.

"Thanks," I said.

The air was sticky but cool against my skin, the wind picking up as the storm moved in. Something about this part of the

Summer Realm set my teeth on edge, like something lurked out there, waiting behind a wall of thorny vines.

I let the shift sweep over me, a shivery blur of magic that, when it ended, left me transformed.

I inhaled deeply. The air smelled of storm and bramble. The earth beneath my paws was rough, but in my puma form, I scarcely noticed.

What I did notice, though, was that the feeling that something was off grew stronger. My shifter intuition was strong, and there was a threat approaching.

I flattened my ears against my head, glancing back at Siobhan.

"Go ahead," she said, nodding. "I'm right behind you."

She ran her hand along my flank, her fingers soft in my rough fur. I wanted to lean into her touch, but my instinct told me we had to move.

I scented the air, not for prey, but for some sense of where the magic was different.

Goddess of wild things, guide me. Show me where we can cross between the worlds.

I inhaled deeply. Exhaled slowly, waiting for the mystical connection between witch and shifter, human and beast, spirit and body, to take root. Earth magic and shifter magic.

Again, I rooted myself, feeling earth against my paws, knowing that in any form I took I was connected to the earth's ancient wildness. Whatever realm I was in, that part didn't change.

Fae realm or human world, it didn't matter. My magic was my own. I saw that now. That was the true lesson. The puma was inside of me, regardless of what form I took. The earth magic of my inner witch was always accessible, wherever I was.

This way, a voice inside of me called.

I followed.

***

Siobhan

Weir in his puma form was a sight to behold. This giant beast made of lanky muscle, leading us on a wending path through a tangled fae wilderness.

The forest we entered was nothing like the one we'd first found ourselves in—not a soft place full of bluebells and ferns, the sort of place where a butterfly or bluebird might perch on an outstretched hand.

This place had a junglelike atmosphere about it, the kind of forest where spiders the size of dinner plates lurked. Every so often, Weir would cast a glance behind him, those gray animal eyes locking with mine, as if to reassure me we were safe.

I rubbed my labradorite pendant for the thousandth time. A birthday gift from my aunt, it was a connection to home, to my family, and to my magical gifts.

Strange how my whole life, I'd wanted freedom from my family. What I wouldn't give now for one of Aunt Fiona's lectures, or my cousin Deirdre fussing about my hair, or a trip to the well for the Rose's guidance.

And though I'd often wondered what my life would be like without my magic—or the burden of the prophecy—now I missed the ever-present song of magic beneath my skin. I longed to take flight on my raven's wings, or to feel the earth's magic tingle beneath my palm.

If Queen Asteria had intended to teach me a lesson, she couldn't have chosen a better way. The lesson, though, probably wasn't the one she'd had in mind.

I called myself to the present, cocking an ear, listening for anything that suggested some shadowy fae creature lurked in the dense underbrush of the forest.

Nothing.

I mean, absolute silence. Aside from our own footfalls and the occasional crackle of leaves or brush under our feet, the forest was dead quiet.

"Weir," I whispered. "Stop."

He turned to me, and our eyes locked briefly. He shook his head, then kept walking.

He sensed it too. But his instinct was to get us out of here, out of a place where there was nowhere we could run—the undergrowth was too dense, so the path was our only way forward.

Then, the rain began to fall in earnest. Thunder rumbled, lightning forking in jagged streaks across the horizon. I didn't know where I ended and the storm began, whether the roar in my ears was rain, thunder, or the rush of blood pounding in my veins.

The path through the jungle-like forest ended, spitting us out in a clearing. The sky was dark as night, though nightfall was still hours away. Lush green grass and vivid red lilies surrounded a temple—stone pillars holding up a roof that must've gleamed like gold when the sun was shining.

Tonight, it looked foreboding, a beautiful place long abandoned, left to be overtaken by the wilderness.

Dripping wet and clutching Weir's clothes to my chest, I ran underneath the shelter of the temple. Weir joined me, shifting back into his human form and quickly stepping into the kilt and shirt.

He grinned at me. "This is it. The place from my vision."

I brushed my sopping-wet hair away from my face. The soggy dress clung tightly to my body, and my nipples beaded against the revealing fabric as Weir's gaze swept over me.

"Did you see a place we could cross through the veil?" I asked, trying to catch my breath. Not from running—that I was used to. But that look he gave me? A look like that would never cease to take my breath away.

"No. But I sense we're close. The energy here is different."

"Why did you shift back?"

"I think I can access my puma's magic in my human form. That's part of how my abilities blend. When I'm a puma, I'm also a witch. And even in my human form, when I'm a witch, I can access the puma's magic."

"Makes sense," I said. "Let's try it. See if you can sense the edge of the veil. Some people describe it as shimmering, like you did. Other people say it feels like cobwebs, or even a waterfall's mist. To me, it's like drawing back a curtain—"

"You got further than I thought you would without your magic, little raven," a voice said.

Weir and I both spun around.

Out of the misty shadows of storm and jungle, stepped Brenna, member of the Summer Queen's Guard. And this time, she'd come armed with something far more dangerous than a dagger or an arrow.

An whirling orb of dark green magic glowed in her outstretched palm, surrounded by a halo of inky shadows.

"Do you know what this is, little raven?" Brenna asked, raising her palm higher, the orb of magic spinning more erratically.

I nodded, trying to speak past the lump in my throat. "Yes, Brenna. I know an elven curse when I see one."

Chapter Thirteen

Weir

I was starting to think that luck wasn't on our side. I stepped forward, my inner puma on high alert. There was a threat in Brenna's stance that hadn't been there when she'd guided us through the halls of the castle.

Or perhaps it had been there, but I'd dismissed it as the nature of her role—a member of the queen's guard would always have to be on alert, after all.

Now, though, whatever disguise she'd worn had fallen away.

"We have until nightfall, Brenna," Siobhan said, taking a small step toward the edge of the temple. "Those were the guidelines Queen Asteria herself put in place. And you've sworn a vow to her."

A grin spread across Brenna's face, something cold and wicked. She shook her head. "I follow the Summer Queen's rules as long as they suit me."

"And now?" Siobhan asked, an edge in her tone, a hint of threat. "What do you think she'll do if you threaten us?"

"She won't know. She'll send someone to collect you, and they'll think you've succeeded in your task. I would've done this earlier, you know. But first, that oaf was with me when I found you in the forest. And I couldn't kill you in the castle. When I found out what punishment the queen had chosen for you, I figured it was my lucky day."

My skin itched. I longed to shift into my puma form, but the orb of magic glistening dark and deadly in her hands held me back. I couldn't risk Siobhan's life, and even in my puma form, no way was I faster than an elven warrior.

Brenna's gaze flicked to me, and she grinned. "Are you confused, little witchling? You shouldn't be meddling in the affairs of the fae."

"We just want to go home," I said. "To our world. I want nothing to do with the affairs of this world. We have our own problems waiting for us back home."

She laughed, the orb spinning wildly where it hovered above her palm. "I'm well aware of the problems that await you. And that nexus of magic—the Crossroads, I believe you call it—was never meant for you. I know it." Her gaze locked on Siobhan, and Brenna stepped closer to us. "And she definitely knows it. Tell him, little raven, little earthbound faerie. Tell him the truth. I've heard the queen and the Rose talking through the sacred well."

I glanced at Siobhan, expecting a nasty retort. Instead her face was pale. She avoided my gaze. "What is she talking about, Siobhan?" I asked.

Siobhan shook her head. "It wasn't my idea. It was the Rose's. She doesn't want humans to have any control over the Crossroads of Magic. That's why the Guardian was able to be captured. Because she was a human gifted with faerie magic, and not a faerie herself. She wants me to help you and the others defeat Weylin. And then the fae will once more take control of the nexus of magic."

"And you weren't going to tell me this? To tell any of us this? Until, what? We'd done everything you wanted us to do?"

I stepped back, putting space between us. The rain picked up, pounding harder on the roof of the temple. Wind whipped the trees. Brenna grinned, seeming impervious to the torrential downpour.

No. No way was I giving that two-faced elf a bit of entertainment.

"It's not that simple," Siobhan said. "You would still have access to the magic. The fae would be its protectors. That's all. But I didn't tell you because..."

"Because they told you not to," I supplied. "And you're a good girl who always does what she's told?"

Brenna laughed, and I immediately regretted letting my emotions get the best of me. I shouldn't have said it.

Siobhan recoiled as though I'd physically slapped her. "No. Not anymore. Not since...I can't explain it. It's different now."

I stepped forward, glaring down at her. "Tell me how."

She stared back at me, but there was no anger in her eyes. "Because of you," she whispered.

"Excellent," Brenna said.

And then she released the orb in her hands.

It struck like lightning, quick and in a blinding flash of light. I flew backwards, hitting one of the stone pillars with enough force that stars danced in my vision.

I struggled to stand. Finally, I crawled toward Siobhan, toward where she lay sprawled on the stone floor.

"Hey," I said. "Come on, Siobhan. Come on."

Her skin was pale, but inky dark green seemed to pulse in her veins.

The stench of ash filled the air.

Gods, no.

Not the vision. Not now. I'd hoped...

What had I hoped? That it could be changed, outsmarted? Hadn't I learned anything from my mother?

"Weir. Thank you. You changed me. But maybe...maybe the Rose was right, and the stars—"

"Screw the stars. What if we've been making our own fates all along?"

She smiled, but there was pain in it. Her hand reached toward my cheek. "Then I have to trust that my fate has been fulfilled. There's no walking away from this. Neither your magic nor mine can stop an elven curse."

I clutched her hand. "Don't say that." There had to be something.

I turned to Brenna. "Undo this. Save her."

Brenna shook her head. "I made him a promise. A deal."

"Who?" I demanded.

Her grin deepened. Freaking psychopath. "Weylin. I take care of her—the daughter of the prophecy, the one who could stop him. And he shares the power of the nexus with me. We'll rule together."

"That's messed up. And you're stupid if you think Weylin Felson will share power with anyone. He killed his own brother, you know. He told us as much."

Brenna shrugged. "I can handle him. Maybe I'll end him before he can end me. I'm tired of working for the royal courts, so close to power, but never able to touch it. I can bend any of the courts to my will with the power of the nexus."

I didn't have time to argue with her or to listen to her insane diatribe. Siobhan needed me. She gasped. The lines of green under her skin were spreading, the curse's poison taking root in her.

A doorway. I had to open a doorway, but to where? Who could be powerful enough to end a curse this strong? And who would be willing to help us?

And then, I knew.

The Rose. Siobhan wasn't just the daughter of the prophecy to the Rose. She was family.

I pressed my hand to the stone, calling on the puma and witch within.

"It doesn't matter, human. Wherever you go, she's going to die."

I ignored Brenna's taunts and pushed on. Then I saw it. The shimmering edge of the veil between the worlds, between human and fae.

"I call to the Rose, ancient fae. Keeper of the Well. One who spoke the prophecy. Siobhan needs you. Come to her aid!" I wasn't sure myself where some of the words came from. An image formed in my head, of a curious being, her skin green and textured like bark, her eyes pools of deepest green. She looked up. And with a feral growl, she shoved the veil aside and stepped through.

***

Siobhan

My body ached as the curse surged through me, its poison seeping into my veins. I'd heard stories about what an elven curse could do to someone, but nothing could've prepared me for this pain.

Vaguely, I heard Weir and Brenna's voices, but everything was starting to sound more distant. The edges of the world pulsed as I blinked, fighting to stay conscious.

Silver light pulsed around us. Was my mind playing tricks on me, or was that real?

And then I saw her. She leaned over me, dark hair in its thick braid interwoven with small rosebuds. She smelled like oakmoss and rain, and the scent was like a balm—familiar, soothing.

The Rose.

"How?" I said.

Her rough palm caressed my forehead, cool against my hot skin. "Oh, sweet little faerie fledgling, my granddaughter many times removed, I only came because he called to me."

"He did?"

"Yes." She pushed my hair away from my face. "The human has more magic in him than even he knows."

"No. This is Queen Asteria's realm. How dare you trespass!" Brenna's voice called. With the Rose present, I felt the curse's hold on me weakening. I managed to sit up. Brenna stepped onto the stone platform of the temple, dripping rainwater, madness glinting in her eyes.

The Rose stood to her full height. "If you harm my children without cause, you cannot expect such rules to apply."

"You'll bring ruin down upon your world, when she finds out—" Brenna taunted, her lips curling into a smug smile.

"It wouldn't be the first time my sister has been angry at me. I'm sure she could find it in her heart to forgive me."

The Rose turned away from Brenna, kneeling before me. "Such a nasty curse, but not the first one I've seen, young one," she said, her voice softer, gentler than I'd ever heard it. I was used to her riddles and her prophecies, her lessons and her instructions. But now, her eyes were the softest green as she gazed down at me.

Her lips formed a song as her hand pressed against my forehead. I didn't know the words—the language was ancient, long forgotten even by most of the earthbound fae. Perhaps, only the Rose herself knew it.

But I felt the kiss of cool rain against my skin, the press of squishy moss beneath my toes. The scent of heather wafted on the air, followed by the most fragrant of roses.

The curse retreated. I felt it draw back into itself, retreating from my veins.

The song ended. In her free hand, the Rose held a tiny pebble, greenish black—the remnant of the curse.

She tossed it aside.

"You are well now, my daughter. Well and safe."

I knew better than to thank the Rose, so I bowed my head. What price would I have to pay for failing her—for stealing the key and betraying the coven whose trust I was supposed to gain, for getting lost in the Summer Realm, for requiring her to cross between the realms and risk incurring the Summer Queen's wrath?

I'd deal with the fact that she and Asteria were related later. My head was already swimming.

I stood on shaky legs. "Weir, we have to get out of here. If we're still here at nightfall..."

Brenna stepped forward. "No. You cheated. I'll explain as much to Queen Asteria."

I turned to Brenna. "You will explain nothing. You are a traitor. What do you think the queen will do to you? You'll be in the dungeons, not us."

"Oh, this wouldn't be the first time I've pulled the wool over the queen's eyes. She, like all who hold power, sees what she wants to see."

"It's true," the Rose said. "This one could easy turn my sister against you. Against me."

Weir came to my side, his arm wrapping around my waist, drawing me to him. I leaned in, grateful for his strength to lean on. He'd worked some high-level magic in order to save me. And the Rose wouldn't have come to just anyone's call. I wondered how he'd managed it.

"What do you think we should do?" Weir asked me.

"We can't let her leave," I said. "I can't have her starting a war between the realms. We already have enough on our plate as it is."

Brenna rolled her eyes. "This is ridiculous."

She turned away, as if to vanish back into the forest and return to the castle to wreak her havoc.

A vine appeared, lashing out and capturing her foot. With a tug, it forced her to the ground. She hit the stone floor with a grunt.

The Rose glared down. "You've betrayed both our realms, so I'm sure my sister will understand what had to be done."

She glanced at Weir. I felt him straighten beside me, a tension seizing his shoulders.

"A mortal with magic. Both man and beast. The ferocity of your cry impressed me, young one. As did your affection for my kin. And your dedication to your task. Your magic runs deeper than even you realize. I wouldn't have heard the call otherwise.

"But you must decide her fate."

I glanced at Weir. His face was pale, his jaw set in grim determination. Would he choose death? The Rose could mete out any fate she wished, however violent.

I didn't dare speak or interfere. If the Rose left Brenna's fate up to Weir, she wouldn't tolerate me interjecting.

"I..." He trailed off, seeming at a loss for words.

"Anything you can imagine, however grim, I can make it so," the Rose said, her tone more warning than promise.

Seconds stretched into minutes as he contemplated. "She betrayed her queen. She tried to kill Siobhan. She tried to end the prophecy for her own selfish gain. I'm a puma shifter. Siobhan is a raven. Let Brenna take on the animal form she deserves."

The Rose nodded, her eyes narrowing to small green slits. "As you will it."

"That's it?" Brenna scoffed, giving a haughty laugh.

"That's it," Weir said, squeezing my waist.

The Rose widened her eyes. "I think...a dung beetle will meet the requirements nicely."

She snapped her fingers. That single snap was all it took.

Brenna, of the Summer Queen's Guard, was no more. A tiny black beetle, slightly shimmering in the dim, gray light, scuttled off, down a crack in the floor of the long-abandoned temple.

The storm was dissipating, stubborn light fighting to break through.

The Rose turned to us. I leaned heavily into Weir, afraid of what was to come. Was I in for a lecture, now that the curse was gone?

"Siobhan, I have been watching you."

"I..."

"Shh," she said. I shushed. "You are more than worthy of the task. All those times I pushed you, chided you, you must know I only wanted you to survive. I wanted to help you be strong enough to complete your task. I suppose I should've offered you more freedom, more encouragement. But the prophecy...I know it weighs upon you. Please know that I cried when I learned of your fate. It wasn't what I wanted for you. But when we learned it...Fiona and I, we knew we had to prepare you. Your parents left because they couldn't bear to watch you meet that fate. I never meant to be cruel. Only to prepare you for the task at hand."

For the first time in my life, she opened her arms to me. I stepped away from Weir's embrace and hugged her. Cool air rustled against my skin, a breeze sweeping over us.

"I understand now," I said.

She smiled. "I'm glad. And you must know that things have come to pass even I did not foresee." She glanced at Weir, admiration in her eyes. "This one, for instance. He will make you a worthy partner. But first, you two have witches to save. And you face a battle in which I cannot intervene. That I and the royals of the faerie realms have vowed to one another. And that is a promise I cannot break."

She clasped my hand, taking Weir's in her other one.

"Follow the Guardian's familiar. She will lead you to where they wait. And know that this is as far as I can take you. It's as far as you need me to take you."

She released our hands and backed away. She turned and, with a sweep of her hand, parted the silvery veil, stepping through and vanishing like a swirl of mist.

"Well, I guess this means I've met your family," Weir said.

I turned to him, grinning. "Oh, that's nothing. Wait until you meet my cousins. And my aunt."

He brushed a kiss against my lips. "Can't wait."

"You say that now," I teased.

A rustling caught both of our attention.

A small owl had landed in the temple, her eyes wide and blinking.

"I guess it's time for you to meet my family," Weir said.

"It looks like it," I agreed.

I tugged the key out from under the top of my dress, where it rested on the chain next to my pendant. "Ready?" I said, squeezing his hand.

He squeezed mine in return. "As I'll ever be."

I felt the shiver of his magic as he made the veil around us visible. A vibrant blue door appeared, swinging open of its own volition.

The owl flew through.

Hand in hand, we followed.

Chapter Fourteen

Weir

An icy gust of wind smacked into me, nearly sent me stumbling backwards.

"Goddess," I said, releasing Siobhan's hand to wrap my arms around myself. "I'd almost forgotten how miserable this place was."

"Here. I can help with that," Siobhan said, smiling up at me.

The green veins of poison that had etched themselves across her skin had vanished. She was her usual self again, though she seemed a little lighter now that she'd talked things out with the Rose.

Siobhan rubbed the labradorite pendant at her throat, her fingers caressing the oval stone. Within seconds, we were both wearing more suitable clothing, each of us in a dark-gray, fur-lined cloak not unlike the one she'd given me when we first met, tumbling together onto the forest floor in the Summer Realm.

Everything had changed since I'd met her—mostly *because* I'd met her. I grinned down at her, planting a kiss on her cheek. "Thank you, faerie lady," I said in my most formal tone.

"You're welcome. Now, let's follow the Guardian's familiar. Let's find your family."

The owl swooped through the snowy forest, scarcely disturbing the snow-covered boughs of the evergreens around us. I vaguely remembered passing through this place when I first escaped the tower, but I'd been running and afraid. So much of that had been a blur. Now, I wondered if the magic of this place, more than my fear of it, was what caused my memory to be so unreliable.

We emerged from the forest, stepping into a wide, snow-covered field. Wind sent swirls of snow spinning like smoke, creating snowdrifts that looked like waves frozen in motion. In the center of the field stood a giant fir tree, easily several stories tall.

The owl landed among its branches, snow cascading down. *Hoo-hoot-hoo-hoo.* She called.

And then she flew away, vanishing mid-flight.

"This isn't right," I said. "There was a tower. I remember it so clearly, the gray stone, the..."

"Weir," Siobhan said, in an exasperated tone. "You're in a faerie realm, remember?"

"Yeah..."

"So?" she said, pointing. "It's glamoured. Look again."

I glanced at the tree. At first, I saw nothing, merely the giant tree standing alone in a barren tundra of a field.

"Seeing through a glamour should be like seeing the edges of the veil between the worlds. Use your gift," she urged.

I did as she'd instructed. At first, nothing. But then, the tree shimmered, flickering in and out of site.

And then I saw it. "That's it. That's the tower."

"Come on," she said, grabbing my hand.

We didn't walk. We ran, hand in hand, plowing through waist-high snowdrifts. I'd be cold later, but right now, sheer adrenaline kept me warm.

We reached the base of the tower. There was a door of worn gray wood, one that I didn't remember being there before.

"Now, we insert the key while saying the incantation," Siobhan said.

"Do you know the incantation?"

She gave me a mildly irritated look—that cocked eyebrow.

"Sorry," I muttered. "Of course you know the incantation."

Her irritation vanished, replaced by a grin.

We were so close. I'd see Mom and Winnie again. We'd all go home.

A thought occurred to me, one that made my stomach churn. "What if he hurt them? What if he punished them for my escape?"

Siobhan squeezed my arm. "We have to believe they're okay. I feel like he's keeping them alive, here for a reason. I don't know what that reason is, but I'm sure he has one."

She was right, but I couldn't shake the dread coiled in my gut.

"Ready?" Siobhan said.

I nodded. Because I was ready. Ready to see my family, my friends, my coven. Ready to go home.

She inserted the key into the lock with a satisfying click.

In a low, somber tone, she spoke the incantation as she turned it.

> *"Beyond the gate*
> *Beyond the root*
> *The tree shall sing*
> *Now look within."*

The door swung open.

I froze, unable to bring myself to enter. So close, yes, but now suddenly I was frozen. What if something terrible had happened to them? The seven of us had become so close during those long months trapped together. Weylin Felson, our captor, had hired a goblin to bring us food. Beyond that, it was a miserable, desperate sort of place.

We stepped inside. The air inside was warmer than outside, but far from warm. The tower wasn't a cozy place to ride out a storm. The main floor was dirt, the floor above, where we'd been kept, rough wood.

I came to the foot of the stairs, my throat dry.

"Come to finish the job?" a female voice called. Ginny, Nick and Evan's grandmother and our coven's high priestess, came to the top of the stairway. She was wrapped in a plain brown blanket, her braid a bit ragged, her skin pale, but otherwise whole.

I couldn't stop myself then.

I ran up the stairs.

I found Winnie first, wrapped in a scratchy blanket. I engulfed her in a bear hug. She sobbed against my shoulder. "I was worried you were dead," she said between sobs.

"Me? No. It would take more than a few blizzards, an encounter with some trolls, and a very angry faerie queen to end your big brother." I tried to keep my voice light, but tears welled up in my eyes anyway.

"I wish I wasn't an empath," she said. "Because then I could pretend you were making that up." A smile played at the edges of her mouth.

I stepped back and studied her. "There's something different about you now," I said. And there was. Always timid and shy, Winnie had a confidence about her. Weylin had tried to break us, but we were still strong.

I hugged Mom.

"Is that her? The woman from the vision?" she asked against my ear, jutting her chin toward Siobhan, who was going from person to person, checking them for signs of injuries.

"That's her," I said, the words coming out breathless.

Fated rightness. That's what I'd thought when I saw the woman in my vision. And it was what I felt every time I was near Siobhan. That was the reason I'd been able to call the Rose.

"Everyone," Siobhan called out. "Weylin was no doubt alerted when we used the key to open the door."

Ginny leaned toward me. "Who is she?"

"This," I said. "Is Siobhan O'Shea, of the earthbound fae. The latest member of the Willow Creek Coven." I smiled at Siobhan. "If she's interested, of course."

Siobhan turned away, but not before I caught the pink tinge in her cheeks. "If they'll have me."

Tricia Dugan, Bailee's grandmother, stepped forward. "If Weir vouches for you, then I'd say we will. Now, come on. I need to see my granddaughter—and check on my roses."

***

Siobhan

I don't know what I'd expected, but a hero's welcome wasn't it. The rescued coven members had quickly enwrapped me in hugs and well wishes. But now came the hard part.

Because I still had to face the coven members I'd stolen from and lied to. Turning into a raven and stealing the key mid-ritual wasn't the best way to earn trust and make new friends.

No. Without a doubt, a much harsher reception awaited me in Willow Creek.

Most of the coven members weren't dressed to brave the elements, so I summoned the doorway right outside of the tower—far enough that its enchantments wouldn't affect my magic, but close enough that they wouldn't have to walk very far.

The sapphire-hued door appeared one more time, cloaked in its aura of silvery light.

I held the door open with my magic as, one by one, the coven members stepped through, out of the Winter Realm where they'd been held captive, and back to the summery warmth of Willow Creek, Virginia.

Weir went through last, and I followed him through with a heavy sigh.

We emerged just steps away from Ginny Saunders's yellow farmhouse.

She let out a sigh of relief as she saw it, falling into her daughter's arms. "I never thought I'd see it again, Maeve," she said.

"Me too, Mama," her daughter said.

The back door of the farmhouse opened, and Nick Felson stepped out, Uncle Mick a few steps behind him.

Nick's gaze fell upon me first, a scowl written on his face.

"Nick!" Maeve called.

And then, it was as though he forgot I existed.

"Mom!" he called, rushing off the porch so fast Uncle Mick had to leap out of the way.

I did my best to blend into the scenery, leaning against a thin birch tree in the backyard as I watched the reunion unfold.

Uncle Mick came to join me. He wrapped a broad arm and my shoulders and pulled me close.

"Prophecy or not, that's a good thing you've done for these people, little raven," he said.

I sniffed. "Do they hate me?"

"No. Nicholas is pissed, but the others seemed to understand once I explained. And now that you've brought them all back together, reunited mother with son, granddaughter with grandchild, brother and sister? Well, you'd be surprised how quickly anger can dissipate after a thing like that. That kind of joy can erase a lot of things."

I nodded. "And what about what's to come?"

"Ah." He rubbed his chin. "Can't say I know a thing about that. But I've seen things in Willow Creek that give me faith. A coven of not just witches, but of shifters and those with faerie blood. People who would walk between worlds to be with the ones they love. And maybe if magic can turn the world upside down, the right kind of magic can make it right-side up again."

Weir strode over, seeming to tear himself away from his family and friends. With a nod, my uncle disappeared into the house, muttering something about needing another cup of tea.

The sun was setting over the mountains, turning the horizon vivid shades of red. I shivered, thinking of the bloodshed that might await us, of the battle to come.

"Are you cold?" Weir asked.

I shook my head. "No. Just worried."

He fell silent. We studied the darkening horizon together, watching the nightfall. "I think we're going to do a bonfire tonight, the whole coven. I hope you'll stay."

"Do they want me to?" I asked, watching the coven members embrace one another, seeming all to talk at once. "All of them?"

"Yeah. I think Nick is starting to understand that you had good intentions. And everyone else already does. And, Siobhan," he said, leaning close, his breath hot against my ear. "I want you to. I don't know what's going to happen tomorrow. Whether we'll survive. Whether any of us—any of this—will be here." He gestured to the group before us, to our surroundings, meaning not just the farm, I knew, but Willow Creek itself. "We all want to have one night of celebration with the ones we love before we face what's to come. And I'd...well, I'd love to have one night with you."

Heat spread through every inch of me, settling at the apex of my legs.

I couldn't think of after. After the battle. After tomorrow. Nothing was certain. Our future lives, our existence, teetered on the brink.

Dusk fell, a bonfire burning bright, cups of tea and mountain pies were served, marshmallows roasted, laughter and song shared. Evan played his guitar, Uncle Mick brought out his mandolin, and we all sang along to "Wild Mountain Thyme" and "The Wild Rover" until our throats ached.

Weir and I snuck away, snagging one of the blankets set by the fire. We found a place on the banks of the creek, with just enough of a break in the canopy of the trees that we could see a smattering of stars.

Our first time together was slow, deliberate, hands exploring every inch of one another until we couldn't take it. He came inside of me, bringing me to ecstasy on the banks of Willow Creek.

I could've spent every night of the rest of my life like that.

If luck and the goddess were on our side, we would have many such nights ahead of us.

***

I hope you enjoyed reading Tangled Spells. *The journey of the Witches of Willow Creek will conclude in the next installment in the series,* Tangled Curses. *Sign up for my author newsletter at www.denisedyoungbooks.com/newsletter to be notified when book 5 becomes available. You'll also receive a free short story,* Fractured Moonlight, *along with other subscriber exclusives!*

About the Author

Equal parts bookworm, flower child, and eclectic witch, Denise D. Young writes fantasy and paranormal romance featuring witches, magic, faeries, and the occasional shifter.

Whatever the flavor of the magic, it's always served with a brisk cup of tea—and the promise of romance varying from sweet to sensual.

She lives with her husband and their animals in an enchanted cottage in the Virginia mountains. She reads tarot cards, collects crystals, gazes at stars, and believes magic is the answer (no matter what the question was).

If you've ever hoped to find a book of spells in a dusty attic, if you suspect every misty forest contains a hidden portal to another realm, or if you don't mind a little darkness before your happily-ever-after, her books might be just the thing you've been waiting for.

***

Find Denise on her web home at www.denisedyoungbooks.com or follow her on BookBub at www.bookbub.com/authors/denise-d-young. For a complete list of all of Denise's books and series, visit www.denisedyoungbooks.com/booklist.
Magic awaits!